WHEN THE MOON WAS BLUE

and other stories

CLIVEDEN PRESS

Published in Great Britain in 1991 by Cliveden Press,
an Egmont Company, Egmont House, PO Box 111,
Great Ducie Street, Manchester M60 3BL.
Printed in the United Kingdom.
ISBN 0 7498 0411 4

Enid Blyton

Enid Blyton was born in London in 1897. Her childhood was spent in Beckenham, Kent, and as a child she began to write poems, stories and plays. She trained to be a teacher but she devoted her whole life to being a children's author. Her first book was a collection of poems for children, published in 1922. In 1926 she began to write a weekly magazine for children called *Sunny Stories*, and it was here that many of her most popular stories and characters first appeared. The magazine was immensely popular and in 1953 it became *The Enid Blyton Magazine*.

She wrote more than 600 books for children and many of her most popular series are still published all over the world. Her books have been translated into over 30 languages. Enid Blyton died in 1968.

Contents

When the moon was blue

One evening, when Jack and Mary were going to bed, they forgot to clean their teeth. Mummy saw their toothbrushes lying beside their tooth-mugs and called to them.

"You naughty children! You haven't cleaned your teeth!"

"We forgot!" said Jack, and the two ran to get their brushes. "Have you ever forgotten to clean your teeth, Mummy?"

"Oh, I daresay I have," said Mummy.

"How often?" asked Mary.

"Oh, once in a blue moon!" said their Mummy, drawing back the curtains so that the air could come into the room.

"What's a blue moon?" said Jack.

"I really don't know," said Mummy.

"Just an ordinary moon turned blue, I expect. I've never seen one."

"You often say things happen 'once in a blue moon'," said Mary. "But a blue moon never comes."

"Well – it might some day!" laughed Mummy. "You'd better be careful then – for goodness knows what might happen if the moon turned blue!"

The children got into bed. Mummy kissed them and said goodnight. Then she turned out the light and went downstairs.

"It's very light out of doors tonight," said Mary. "The moon must be up."

"Daddy said it would be a full moon tonight," said Jack. "Oh, Mary – wouldn't it be exciting if it was blue!"

"Yes, but it won't be," said Mary sleepily. "Things like that never seem to happen. Think how often we've tried to see fairies and never have – and how often we've wished wishes and they haven't come true – and tried to work spells and they won't work. I don't believe in those things any more!"

"I still do," said Jack, "because once one of my wishes really did come true."

"Well, it must have been an accident, then," said Mary, yawning. "Goodnight, Jack. I'm going to sleep."

Both children fell fast asleep in a minute or two. They slept soundly, and didn't hear the wardrobe creaking loudly. They didn't hear the cat mewing outside either.

But when twelve o'clock struck, they did hear something. At least Jack did. He heard an owl hooting outside the window, and he opened his eyes.

"Wit-wit!" said the owl, "woo-wit-wit!"

Jack sat up and wondered what time it was. He looked at the window. A good deal of light came in from outside, for the moon was full. It had gone behind a cloud for a moment, quite a small one, for Jack could see the moon skimming along behind it. He watched it, waiting for it to come out again.

And when it did he gasped and stared

and rubbed his eyes – for what do you suppose? Why, the big round moon was as blue as forget-me-nots! There it shone in the sky, looking very peculiar indeed.

"There's a blue moon!" cried Jack. "Mary, Mary, wake up! There's a blue moon!"

Mary woke up with a jump and sat up. She stared at the moon in the greatest surprise.

"So there is!" she said. "Oh, Jack – do you suppose anything extraordinary will happen? Oh, do let's go to the window and see if we can spy any fairies or pixies about. Mummy said we might see them once in a blue moon!"

They ran to the window – and looked down their moonlit garden. But not a fairy or pixie could they see.

"Let's wish a few wishes!" said Jack, gazing up at the bright blue moon. "They might come true now the moon is blue."

"Yes, let's," said Mary. "I wish we could see a fairy or a gnome or something!"

"And I wish we could, too!" said Jack.

And immediately they did! A gnome, very small and bent, ran out from under the lilac bush in the middle of the garden, and went to the little round pool. In the middle of this was a little statue of a bunny, sitting on a big flat stone.

The gnome jumped over the water and landed beside the bunny. At once the stone rabbit took his hand and stood up. The gnome began to pull at the flat stone on which the bunny had been sitting – and before the children's very eyes, he suddenly disappeared! The stone bunny sat down again and made no movement.

"Did you see that, Mary?" cried Jack. "Come on, quickly! We'll see where he disappeared to. Put on your dressing-gown and I'll put on mine."

They threw on their dressing-gowns

and ran quietly down the stairs. Out they went into the garden and ran to the pond. With a leap Jack was over the water and standing beside the stone bunny in the middle of the pond. To his enormous surprise, the small rabbit at once put a cold paw into his hand and got up. Jack turned to the flat stone – and saw an iron ring on it, and the stone came up. Under it lay a steep stone stairway!

"Come on, Mary!" cried Jack. "Here's an adventure for us! We've always wanted one!"

Mary jumped over the water beside Jack, and peered down the steps. The stone rabbit put its other paw into her hand, and looked beseechingly at her.

"This little rabbit's alive, although it's just a statue!" said Mary, in surprise. "Can you speak, Bunny?"

"Yes," said the rabbit. "I can speak once in a blue moon – and the moon is blue tonight!"

"Are you really a statue or are you alive?" asked Jack.

"I was once the first rabbit in the carriage of the Princess Philomela of Heylo Land," said the bunny. "But one night the wicked gnome Twisty lay in wait for her carriage — and put a log in our path. So over I went and all the other three rabbits, and the Princess fell out of the carriage. The gnome picked her up and carried her off — and turned me and the other rabbits into stone. He sold us for the middles of ponds and there we stayed!"

"Goodness me!" said Jack, in the greatest surprise. "Whoever would have thought of such a thing? Where is the Princess now?"

"I don't know," said the rabbit, mournfully. "She's still a prisoner somewhere, I expect. The gnome has a secret way to Fairyland down that stairway. He may have gone to the Princess now."

"Well, let's go after him then!" said

Jack. "We may see where he keeps the Princess, and perhaps be able to rescue her! Will you come with us, Bunny?"

"Yes, but I'm made of stone, and I would make so much noise!" said the rabbit.

"I'll wish you alive again!" said Jack. "It seems as if wishes come true once in a blue moon!"

"Yes, wish!" said Mary. So Jack wished hard.

"I wish this stone bunny may come alive!" he said – and immediately his wish came true! The little rabbit grew soft and warm and furry – and whiskers grew out of his cheeks. The stone bunny had had no whiskers at all.

"I'm alive. I'm alive!" he cried, frisking round and nearly falling into the pond.

"Mind! You'll fall in the water!" said Mary, clutching hold of the excited bunny. "Come along. We'll go down the steps now."

So down the steps they all went, Jack first, then the bunny, then Mary. It was dark when they got to the bottom, but a lamp hung a little way farther on, and showed them a narrow passage. They went along, most excited.

After a while they came to a turnstile, and they pushed against it. It wouldn't turn round, and Jack thought they had better climb over it. But before he could do so, a small brownie popped his head out of a window in the wall of the passage and said: "Penny each, please."

"We haven't any pennies," said Jack. "We are in our dressing-gowns, and we don't keep pennies there. Please let us through. Has the Twisty Gnome gone this way?"

"Yes, he has," said the brownie, nodding his head. "He often goes this way. No one else goes, except myself – and I only go once in a blue moon!"

"Well, it's a blue moon tonight!" said Jack. "We've seen it!"

"What!" cried the brownie, his face full of excitement. "The moon is blue! My stars, I must go and look!"

He squeezed himself through the window in the wall of the passage, pushed past Jack, Mary and the rabbit and disappeared up the tunnel.

"Come on, let's climb over, now he's gone!" said Mary. So they all climbed over the turnstile, and went on down the tunnel again. But it didn't go very far this time. It opened out into a cave through which a dark, swift river ran. A little pixie sat by the side of some boats, half-asleep.

"Wake up!" cried Jack, running to him. "Has the Twisty Gnome gone this way?"

"Yes, down the river," said the pixie, in surprise. "But he said I was to let no one else but him have my boats today."

"Oh, well, it can't matter once in a blue moon!" said Jack, getting into one.

"What, is the moon blue?" cried the pixie, in delight. "Oh, have my boats then, have them all if you want to! I'm going up to see the moon, the moon, the moon!"

He sat down on a big toadstool growing nearby, and, to the children's great amazement, shot upwards at a great speed.

"Well, I suppose he's gone to see the moon, like the brownie," said Jack. "Come on, Mary and Bunny! We mustn't let the Twisty Gnome get too far ahead!"

They set off in the boat. Jack steered, but there was no need for oars, for the river was very strong and took them along itself. In a few minutes it came out into the open air, and there, hanging in the sky, was the moon, still as blue as forget-me-nots!

As the boat went along, Jack caught sight of a large notice on one of the banks. He looked at it. To his great surprise, it had one word on it:

JUMP!

"Jump," said Jack, puzzled; "why jump?"

"Oh, look!" cried Mary, pointing

ahead. "There is a waterfall or something coming. Jack, if we don't jump, we shall go over the falls. Oh, I'm frightened!"

"Come with me," the bunny said. He took the strings from Jack and pulled the boat towards the bank. It ran into it with a bump, and at the same time all three jumped out! They landed on the soft grass and rolled over. Just ahead of them the river shot over the falls with a roar. Their boat spun round once and then headed for the waterfall. Over it went, and that was the last they saw of it!

"Goodness! I hope this sort of thing only happens once in a blue moon!" said Jack.

"Oh, it does," said the bunny. "Come on. Do you see that castle over there? I am sure that is where the gnome has gone. It belongs to him. Perhaps he has the Princess Philomela locked up in one of the rooms."

They all set off for the castle. They

soon arrived there, and looked up at it. It was very big, and had hundreds of windows, and a great wooden door.

"I don't think I want to go in that door," said Mary. "It looks as if it might shut behind us and make us prisoners in the castle, too. Isn't there another way of getting in?"

"We'll spy round and see," said Jack. So they walked all round the castle – and right at the back they discovered a very small door, painted a bright yellow. Jack pushed it – and it came open!

He and the others peeped inside. It led into a great yard. They all went inside and looked round. The kitchen door stood open and a smell of cakes being baked came out.

"Come on," said Jack. "We may be able to sneak inside."

He crept up to the kitchen door – and at that moment a large gnome-woman came to it to shake a duster. She stared at the three in surprise. They didn't know what to say.

"Oh," she said at last. "I suppose you have come with a message for the Twisty Gnome. You are not the washing, are you? Or the baker?"

"Oh, no!" said Jack. "May we go inside and see the gnome?"

Mary was horrified to hear Jack ask this, for she certainly didn't want to see the horrid Twisty Gnome, in case they were all taken prisoners. The gnome servant nodded her head.

"He's just upstairs with the Princess," she said. "But he won't be long. Come and wait in the hall."

She took them inside and led them to a great hall. They sat down on a bench and she disappeared back into the kitchen.

"Did you hear that?" said Jack. "She said the Twisty Gnome was upstairs with the Princess! So she *is* here! We'll rescue her! Come on — we must hide before the gnome comes back. I don't want to see him, of course — that was only an excuse to get inside!"

Jack, Mary and the rabbit looked round to see where they could hide. There was a long curtain hanging at the foot of the stairs, and the three crept behind it. They hadn't been there more than a minute or two when they heard footsteps coming down the stairs. It was the Twisty Gnome.

As he came into the hall, the gnome-woman ran out. "Master," she said, "there are three . . ."

She stopped short and looked round in surprise – for she could not see Mary, Jack or the bunny. "How strange!" she said. "A boy and a girl and a rabbit came to see you. They were here just now!"

"Oh, indeed!" said Twisty, in a hoarse and threatening voice. "They were here, were they? Well, where are they now? I suppose you've let them go into my magic room, and disturb my spells. Grrrrrr! If you have, I'll turn you into a dustbin lid. That's all you're fit for!"

"Oh, Master, I don't think they've gone into your magic room!" cried the servant – but the gnome had disappeared into a little room on the opposite side of the hall. The servant followed – and in a trice Mary, Jack and the rabbit slipped out from the curtain and were running upstairs as fast as they could.

At each landing there was a locked door. Jack stopped outside each one and called softly.

"Princess Philomela! Are you there?"

But there was no reply at all until he reached the topmost room of all – and then an answer came, in a soft, eager voice.

"Yes, yes! I am here! Who is it?"

The door was locked and bolted – but the key was in the lock. Jack turned it, and then undid the bolts. He opened the door – and saw inside the room a beautiful little princess with long golden hair waving round her face, and the brightest blue eyes he had ever seen.

"Oh, oh, you've come to rescue me!"

cried Philomela, and she gave Jack and Mary a tight hug each. She saw the bunny and clapped her hands in delight.

"Why, you are dear little Whiskers, one of the bunnies that used to pull my carriage!" she said, and she lifted him up and kissed him. "I suppose you brought these children here to save me."

"We must go, Princess," said Jack. "The gnome knows we are here. He is looking for us downstairs. He may come up at any minute."

"Come along then," said Philomela.

So they all began to creep down the stairs and at last came to the hall. No one was there. Not a sound was to be heard. Every door that led into the hall was shut.

"I say!" said Jack. "I don't remember which door led into the kitchen, do you?"

"We don't need to go that way," said Mary. "What about trying the front door?"

"No," said Jack. "It's too big and

heavy. It would make a noise. Let's go into one of the rooms; it doesn't much matter which one so long as the gnome isn't there, and then climb out of the window. That should be easy."

So they listened outside the nearest door, and, not hearing the tiniest sound from inside, they pushed open the door and slipped into the room. They ran to some curtains and pulled them aside to get at the windows – but alas – there were no windows at all!

Then they heard the sound of a key being turned in the lock – and looked round to see the Twisty Gnome looking at them with a very nasty grin.

"Ha!" he said. "So you thought you would rescue the Princess and all escape very nicely, did you? Well, you made a mistake, I'm afraid. I have four prisoners now, instead of one!"

He went to the middle of the floor, and pulled up a small wooden trap-door.

"Get down into my cellar," he said. "There is no escape from there. It is

dark and cold and full of spiders. You will enjoy a night or two there, I am sure!"

The Princess began to cry. Jack and Mary looked fierce, but could do nothing. The bunny slipped down into the cellar without a word.

When they were all in the dark, damp cellar, the gnome shut the trap-door with a bang and bolted it. They heard his footsteps going out of the room above.

"What are we going to do?" sobbed Philomela. "Oh, I am so frightened."

"So am I!" said Mary, wiping her eyes.

"There's no need to be," said the rabbit, in a soft voice. "I can rescue you all. I am a bunny, you know, and my paws are good for digging holes. This cellar is in the ground – there is earth all around. It will not take me long to dig my way out. Then I will fetch many more rabbits and we will all dig together."

"Splendid idea!" cried Jack. The

rabbit at once began to scrape in the
earth. Soon he had made quite a tunnel,
and the earth was piled in the cellar. In
a few minutes he had disappeared – and
before long he had fetched fifteen more
rabbits, who all dug and scraped away
valiantly.

"Now I think the tunnel is big
enough," said the rabbit. And so it
was. Jack, Mary and Philomela easily
made their way up it, and came out at
the side of the big castle!

"The rabbits have brought a carriage
for you, Your Highness," said the little
bunny – and there, sure enough, was
a shining silver carriage! Four rabbits
stood ready to pull it, and the Princess
got in.

"You must come, too," she said to the
children – but just as they were about
to get in, a peculiar thing happened.

"Look at the moon!" cried the rabbit,
and pointed to where the moon was
slowly sinking down the sky.

Everyone looked. It was turning

bright yellow! Yes – there was no mistake about it. All its blue colour was fading – and even as they watched, it was all gone, and there was the moon, as bright yellow as a daffodil, filling the sky with light.

"The blue moon's gone," said the rabbit sadly. "It's gone – but we've rescued the Princess!"

A strange wind blew up at that moment and the children suddenly felt giddy. There came a loud humming noise. Jack and Mary sat down on the grass and shut their eyes, for they felt very strange.

After a while the humming noise died away – and they opened their eyes.

Will you believe it? They were back in their beds again! Yes, they were – both of them sitting up and gazing out of the window at the moon, which was yellow, and shining brightly!

"Mary!" cried Jack. "Did we dream it all?"

"No, we couldn't have," said Mary. "It

was all so real. The moon really *was* blue!"

"Well, tomorrow we will look for that trap-door again, where the bunny was," said Jack, lying down. "Then we will know for certain it was all true. How funny – Daddy will wonder where the stone bunny is gone, won't he?"

But do you know, when the morning came, the stone bunny was back again. Yes, he was – standing in the middle of the pond on the big flat stone just as before.

"But the trap-door is underneath him, Daddy," said Mary, earnestly, after she had told Daddy all about their very strange adventure. "It really is. Will you take him off the stone and see?"

"No," said Daddy. "He is cemented to the stone. I'm not going to move him. You dreamt it all!"

Well, isn't that a pity? If only Daddy would move the rabbit, and let the children find that trap-door again, they would know that it wasn't a dream. But Daddy won't.

Perhaps *you* will see a blue moon one day. If you do, wish a wish – for it is sure to come true, once in a blue moon!

Jane goes out to stay

Jane was going to stay with her friend Pam. She felt very grown-up indeed. She had never been away from home before – but here she was, watching Mummy pack a little bag with her nightdress and dressing-gown, her flannel, sponge and toothbrush, and a clean dress.

"Shall I pack Bunny for you?" said Mummy.

"Oh, *no*," said Jane. "I know he sleeps with me every night, Mummy, but I'm too big to take a bunny away with me. Pam would laugh at me."

"No, she wouldn't. Pam is a year younger than you are, and I expect she takes a toy to bed with her every

single night," said Mummy. "Very well. I won't put Bunny in."

Jane thought of all the things she would tell Pam. She wanted to make Pam think she was very grown-up and important. She would say, "Pam, do you know this – Pam, do you know that?" and Pam would listen eagerly.

She arrived at Pam's in time for dinner. Pam hugged her, because she liked Jane very much.

"Do you mind being away from home?" she said. "Will you like staying with me? I've never stayed away even one night without Mummy."

"Ah, but I'm older than you," said Jane. "I'm in a class higher at school, too. I shan't mind staying away from home a bit!"

They had dinner, and then they went out to play. The dog next door barked, and made Pam jump.

"Are you afraid of dogs?" said Jane. "I've got a dog of my own at home. Can you ride?"

"No, I can't. Can you?" asked Pam.

"Oh, yes. I ride every Saturday, on a big, white pony called Sweetie," said Jane. "I gallop. And once I went so fast that everyone thought my pony was running away. But he wasn't."

"You must be very clever," said Pam. "I wish I could do things like that."

Jane chose all the games, and she chose ones she was quite the best in. She could run faster than Pam, and she could jump higher.

"Mummy, Jane is wonderful," said Pam, when they went in to tea. "She does everything so well. And she's not a bit afraid of dogs or horses – or of tigers, either, are you, Jane?"

"I don't expect I would be, if I met one," said Jane, pleased at all this praise. "I like animals. You ought to like animals, too, Pam, then you wouldn't be so scared when you see a big dog, or hear a cow moo."

After tea they played card games. Jane was much quicker at them than

Pam. She 'Snapped' everything, and won four games straight off. Pam looked a little sad.

"I wish I could win once," she said.

"Have a game of Happy Families. You may win then," said her mother, feeling rather sorry for the smaller girl. She thought that Jane might just let Pam win once, to please her. But no, Jane won Happy Families, too.

"I'm stupid, aren't I?" said poor Pam, almost in tears. "I wish I was as wonderful as Jane, Mummy. She can do everything. Jane, do you ever cry?"

"Oh, no," said Jane. But this wasn't quite true. She did cry sometimes.

"Not even when you fall down and hurt your knee?" asked Pam.

"Of *course* not!" said Jane.

"Are you ever frightened in the night?" said Pam. "Because I am."

"Of *course* I'm not," said Jane, in a scornful voice. "I just go to sleep, and don't bother about anything, not even thunder."

"You're too good to be true, Jane, dear," said Pam's Mummy. "And now I think it's bedtime. Hurry up and have a nice hot bath, because it's very cold tonight."

Soon the two little girls were in separate little beds, drinking a nice warm glass of milk. Then Pam's mother said good night to them both, and went downstairs.

She came up a little later with Pam's hot water bottle, and one for Jane, too. But Jane was already fast asleep. So very gently Pam's mother pushed the hot water bottle, in its soft furry cover, down into the bed beside the sleeping Jane. Jane never had a hot water bottle at home, and had not asked for one.

About three hours later Jane woke up. She felt a warm patch against her legs. Whatever could it be? She put down her hand and felt it. It was soft and furry and warm. It must be some animal that had crept into bed with her when she was asleep!

"Go away!" said Jane, and kicked out at it. But it didn't move. It just lay against her leg, furry and warm. Jane felt suddenly frightened.

She sat up in bed and shouted. "Help! Help! There's a wild animal in bed with me! It's biting me, it's biting me, help, help!"

Pam woke up with a jump. She switched on the light and stared at Jane. "Oh, Pam! There's a horrid wild animal in bed with me!" cried Jane again. "It'll bite me to bits! I believe it's nibbling me now! Oh! OHHHHH!"

"I'll save you, I'll save you!" cried Pam, and she jumped out of bed. She pulled Jane right out of bed, and then threw back the covers. She saw the furry hot water bottle cover, and bent to pick it up and throw it away, thinking it was some animal.

Then she saw what it was. How she stared! Then she laughed. She had a very merry little laugh, that went ha-ha-ha-ho-ho-ho, he-he. She rolled on

Jane's bed and she laughed till the tears came into her eyes.

"What's the matter, Pam?" asked Jane, upset. But Pam was laughing too much to tell her. Then in came Pam's mother to see what all the noise was about.

"Oh, Mummy, oh, Mummy! Jane was so funny!" said Pam. "She screamed and shouted and cried because she said she had a wild animal in her bed that was biting her to bits! And I got out to rescue her from the dreadful animal – and it was only her hot water bottle!"

Then it was Mummy's turn to laugh. "Well, well, well – to think of our brave and wonderful Jane being scared of a hot water bottle! I slipped it into your bed, dear, when you were asleep."

Poor Jane! She did feel so very, very silly. To think she had yelled like that over a hot water bottle.

She got back into bed, very red in the face. She threw the hot water bottle out on the floor.

"Now don't be cross as well as foolish, Jane," said Pam's mother. "It really was very funny, you know, and we couldn't help laughing. And don't you think little Pam was brave, to jump out of bed and come and try to save you from the wild animal you were shouting about?"

"Yes. She was brave," said Jane. "Thank you, Pam. You're braver than I am!"

Then they went to sleep. But you won't be surprised to hear that next day Jane was much nicer to Pam, and even let her win two games of Snap!

"It's my birthday"

Jib the brownie hadn't a proper house. He lived in a snug little tent that he had made out of the big leaves of the chestnut tree. He just sewed them together and, lo and behold, he had a nice little tent.

He used to live for a few days in one place and then roll up his tent, tie it on his back and go off to another village. And in every place he pitched his tent, he would say the same thing.

"It's my birthday tomorrow!"

Then he would sigh and look sad, and the people round him would say, "Why do you look sad?"

And Jib would say, "Well, it's sad to be away from home and my friends and have a birthday – no presents, no cards, nothing!"

Well, the pixies and elves were kind little people and you can guess what they did!

"Let's go and buy Jib birthday cards and some little presents!" they would say, and off they would go at once.

And the next day Jib would have lovely cards and all kinds of nice little presents. The little folk would beam at him and wonder if he would give a birthday party and ask them all to it.

But he never did. On that very afternoon he would quietly fold up his chestnut-leaf tent and steal away; and when a pixie came by, no Jib and no tent were there! That was really very mean of him.

One day he came to the village of Ho. It was full of brownies like himself, and pixies and elves. Jib put up his little tent, and people came to call.

"My name's Jib," he said. "I hope you don't mind my staying here in my tent.

It seems such a nice place and such nice people."

"Oh, we like to make strangers welcome," said Boff, a big, burly brownie with a very long beard. "We hope you'll be happy here."

Jib hung his head and looked sad. "I expect I *shall* be happy soon," he said, "but just now I feel rather miserable. You see – it's my birthday tomorrow – and it's sad to be far from home and have no cards and no presents."

"Dear me – we must do something about *that*," said kind Mrs Boff. She and Boff went off, talking together, and Jib grinned to himself. Now he would have plenty of cards and heaps of presents.

"I shall leave tomorrow afternoon, and go to Cherry Village and sell all the presents," he said to himself. "I shall get a nice lot of money for them. How very stupid people are, to be sure!"

Mr and Mrs Boff went round the village of Ho, telling everyone that Jib was having a birthday the next day and people must try and make it nice for him.

"Hm!" said Old Wily the goblin. "I don't much like the look of that fellow, Jib. Why should we spend money on him? Would he spend any on us?"

"Oh, he's sure to have a little party and ask us all to it," said Mrs Boff. "He'll be so pleased with his cards and presents, he'll surely want to do something nice in return."

Old Wily didn't think that a brownie with a mean face like Jib's would ever want to do anything nice for anyone. He sat and thought for a little while, and then he put on his old hat and went to visit his cousin, Old Sly. There wasn't much that Old Sly didn't know. He had lived a long time and he had heard a lot and knew a lot. He was two hundred years old and his beard had grown down to his feet and round his ankles.

"Ever heard of anyone called Jib?" asked Old Wily.

Old Sly frowned and thought for a

long while. "Ah, yes," he said at last.
"He's the fellow who goes round with
a chestnut-leaf tent and says he's
miserable because it's his birthday and
he's far from home. Then he collects a
whole lot of presents and sells them
in the next village. A very unpleasant
fellow."

"Thank you, Old Sly," said Old Wily.
"Exactly what I thought." Off he went
back to the village of Ho, thinking hard.
He found that everyone had bought a
card or a present for Jib.

Old Wily went to visit the baker.
"It's Mr Jib's birthday tomorrow," he
said. "And he wants to have a nice
little party. Will you arrange it, please?
Birthday cake and buns and sandwiches
and ice-creams and biscuits and jellies
and balloons and crackers. All the very
best, of course."

"Certainly, certainly," said the baker,
delighted, and he set to work.

Well, next day Jib sat in his tent and
waited for the little folk to bring him

cards and presents. And as usual they did! Dear me, what a lot of money they had spent on that rascal Jib.

"*So* kind of you!" he kept saying. "So very kind! Thank you, thank you!"

"He hasn't said anything about a party yet," whispered Mrs Boff.

"Oh, there'll be a party," said Old Wily. "Yes, yes – there's sure to be a party. A fine one, too. I've seen the baker icing a splendid birthday cake."

Well, Jib heard this, as Old Wily meant that he should, and he was delighted. "What! A party as well as all these presents," he thought. "Magnificent!"

So he didn't fold up his chestnut-leaf tent and steal away as he usually did. He waited for the party!

It was a very fine party indeed. The birthday cake was made in the shape of a white palace and really looked lovely. Everyone had two pieces. Jib had three, and goodness knows how many cakes and buns and ice-creams he had as well.

And after the party, when everyone was saying goodbye, the baker came up and bowed. "I hope everything was all right, Mr Jib," he said.

"Perfectly," said Jib. "Couldn't be better."

"I'm glad," said the baker and unrolled a long sheet of paper. "Here's the bill."

What a bill it was! Jib stared in horror. What! All that money for a party. Well, *he* wasn't going to pay for it!

"I'm not paying that," he said, roughly.

"But it was *your* birthday party!" said Old Wily, who had put himself nearby. "Surely you gave it in return for the kindness of all these people? Surely, Jib, you didn't mean to fold up your tent and go without paying the bill? Oh, surely not! Where is Mr Plod the policeman? Let us ask him if that would be a right thing to do."

Jib looked very scared. He didn't like

policemen. He was always afraid they would find out all his mean little tricks. He hurriedly put his hand into his pocket, and pulled out a very fat purse. He paid the baker's bill without a word.

"That was wise of you, Jib, very wise," said Old Wily. "I hope you will *always* pay for birthday parties on the many birthdays you have each year. Will you, Jib?"

Jib began to tremble. He waited till everyone had gone then he packed up his tent quickly. Old Wily watched him go. "I'm coming to your next birthday party!" he called. "Let me see now – when is your next birthday, Jib? Next week, I suppose. I'll be there!"

Jib went hurrying off without a word, and so far as I know he hasn't had a birthday since! What a way to go on, wasn't it?

The Tom Thumb fairies

Once upon a time there were some very small creatures called Tom Thumb fairies – so small that you could easily hold a hundred in the palm of your hand and hardly feel any weight.

They lived in some little red toadstools in Toadstool Village on the borders of Fairyland. The toadstools were small enough, goodness knows, but the fairies were so tiny that each toadstool was as big as a house to them. So they hung curtains at the windows in the top, and had a little door in the stalk with a knocker and a letter-box, just as you have.

Now one night there came a band of red goblins creeping round Toadstool

Village. It was a dark night and there were so many clouds that not even the stars gave their faint light. The goblin chief gave a signal, and at once two goblins went to each toadstool house, opened the door and captured the small fairy inside the bedroom at the top of the toadstool.

Nobody heard them squeal. Nobody heard them struggle. They were popped into bags and taken off to Goblin Town at once, there to wait on the goblins and help them with their spells. Their wings were clipped off, so that they could not fly home. The wings grew again in a few weeks' time, but every time they grew the goblins clipped them off again.

The Tom Thumb fairies were very unhappy. "What shall we do?" they wept. "We hate working underground all day long. We hate these red goblins, who are so unkind. We don't know the way home. We have no wings to fly with."

One day one of the Tom Thumb

fairies found a worm-hole leading up to the sunlight. She was overjoyed, and she whispered the news to the others.

"One morning when the goblins have gone off somewhere, we will creep up this worm-hole and escape," said the fairy.

"But the goblins will come after us," said the others. "We shan't know which way to go when we get up into daylight again."

"Never mind," said the first one. "We will see what we can do."

So the next time the red goblins went off together, leaving the Tom Thumb fairies to do all the work, the tiny creatures began to make their way up the worm-hole. It was very small – but they were smaller still.

Soon they came to the worm, and they could not get by, for the worm was fat and lay squeezed up in its bedroom – a large part of the hole halfway down the passage.

"Please move up a bit," said one of the

Tom Thumbs, poking the worm. "We want to get by."

The worm moved up its hole. It put out its head and listened, for it had no eyes to see with. Was any sharp-eyed bird about? No – it could hear no pattering of feet. So it drew itself right up and let the fairies use its rather slimy hole as a passage up to the daylight.

How pleased the Tom Thumbs were when they saw the bright sunshine again! "Now we must plan what to do," they cried.

"Get back into your hole," shouted a fairy to the worm. "The red goblins may come after us. Don't you move out of your hole for them, or they will catch us."

"There are plenty of other holes for the red goblins to come up by," said the worm, sliding back again. "There's the mouse-hole just over there – and the big rabbit-hole in the hedge – and any amount of empty worm-holes too."

"Oh dear!" said the Tom Thumbs, looking round as if they expected to see the red goblins at any moment. "We had better find a hiding-place in case they come. Where can we go?"

There were pink-tipped daisies about – much, much bigger than the Tom Thumb fairies. There was a large dandelion plant too, with great golden blossoms.

"I will hide you," said the dandelion in a soft silky voice. "You are so tiny that you can each slip under one of my many golden petals. Hurry now, for I can hear the red goblins coming."

In a trice the Tom Thumbs had run to the large dandelion, which spread its hundreds of soft petals to the sun. Each fairy lifted up a silken petal and slipped underneath. There they hid in safety whilst the red goblins, suddenly appearing from the mouse-hole, began to hunt for the Tom Thumbs.

"They must be somewhere about,"

shouted the chief one. "Hunt well, all of you."

Well, they hunted and they hunted, but no one thought of looking in the dandelion-head. There the Tom Thumbs hid, and did not make a movement for fear of being found.

"Well, goblins, we must get back to our home underground," said the chief at last. "But you, Gobo, and you, Feefo, and you, Huggo, stay up here and keep watch, in case those Tom Thumbs are hiding anywhere."

The goblins went back down the mouse-hole, but Gobo, Feefo and Huggo stayed behind, their sharp black eyes looking round and about. The Tom Thumbs did not dare to move.

"Don't you worry," whispered the dandelion. "You have a soft bed – and if you look hard you will find honey to eat, and when the night comes you will have dew to drink. Keep still and rest, and you will be safe."

Day after day the Tom Thumbs lay

hidden in the golden dandelion, whilst the three goblins kept a strict watch. The dandelion grew on its stalk and lifted the Tom Thumbs higher – and then something odd happened.

It was time for the golden dandelion-head to fade. The gold left it – it closed up like a bud once more, holding the Tom Thumbs safely inside. It was no longer a wide golden flower, but a rather untidy-looking dead one, tightly shut. It drooped its head so low that it hid it amongst the leaves. Still the Tom Thumbs lay hidden – because now they could not get out!

What would happen to them? They did not know. The honey was almost finished, and the dew no longer fell on to them for drink. They huddled together in the dead flower, frightened and miserable.

The stalk of the dandelion grew longer and longer. How strange! But it had a reason. Yes – for the flower was turning into seed – and when that seed was ready it must be taken up into the air on a long, long stalk so that the wind might blow it away. Oh, clever dandelion!

So it came about that one day the dead dandelion raised its head again, on its long, long stalk. It stood straight up once more, and – wonder of wonders! – instead of a golden head it now had a head full of marvellous white seeds. It was a beautiful dandelion clock.

And now the Tom Thumb fairies began to get excited. "Look!" they cried. "The dandelion has grown us little parachutes! Do look! There is one for each of us. We can hold on to the stalk – it is like a handle for us – and when the wind blows, the parachute of hairs will carry us far, far away from here, safe from the red goblins."

But the wind did not blow them away – someone else did. Who was that? Well, it may have been you! A little girl came down that way and saw the dandelion clock standing there, so tall and beautiful. She did not see the three red goblins still keeping a sharp watch. She picked the dandelion clock and looked at it.

"I shall blow you," she said. "I want to know the time. Now then – PUFF! – one o'clock. PUFF! – two o'clock. PUFF! – three o'clock. PUFF! – four o'clock. PUFF! – five o'clock. Oh, it's tea-time! I must hurry."

She ran off, pleased to see the pretty seeds blowing in the air – but she didn't see that each one carried a Tom Thumb fairy.

The dandelion seeds flew high and far. When at last they came to the ground they were far, far away from the red goblins' home. The Tom Thumbs took the first bus home they could find; and now they are safe in Toadstool Village again – and at night they all lock and bolt their doors!

Wasn't it lucky for them that they hid in a dandelion?

Midnight tea party

I peeped one night in the
    playroom,
And I was surprised to see
The pussycat and the teddy
Having their friends to tea!

The clockwork mouse and old Jumbo,
The sailor doll and the clown,
And all the dolls from the dolls' house
At the table were sitting down.

Pussy had borrowed my tea set,
And Teddy was cutting a cake,
There were jellies a-shake in the dishes,
And crackers for each one to take.

You think I was dreaming? I wasn't!
Today I found crumbs on the mat,
And jelly in one of the dishes,
And the pussycat's blue paper hat!

The big black cat

The big black cat from across the road used to sit on the wall and wait for Joan and Richard to come back from school.

He stood up and arched his back when he saw them coming. They ran up to him and stroked him, tickling his soft neck.

"You're a very nice cat," said Joan. "If you come into our garden this afternoon I'll give you a bit of fish. We're having fish for dinner, so there's sure to be a bit of skin for you off our plates."

The cat strolled into their garden almost every day. Sometimes the children gave him milk or little tit-bits. Sometimes they played with him, and

once he even went to sleep in Joan's doll's pram. That made Mummy laugh.

"Just look at that cat!" she said. "Anyone would think he belonged to you two children, not to Mrs Brown across the road."

The cat loved playing with the children's toys. He played ball very well. He liked running after Richard's clockwork train. He patted all the little dolls that sat in the train when they went for a ride.

Whenever he saw the children playing he went out to play with them. "Hallo, Blackie!" they would say, when he strolled into the garden. "Come along and play!"

But one day Richard played with something that Blackie couldn't catch or chase. He had a new aeroplane!

It was a lovely thing. It really could fly beautifully. It had to be wound up tightly with elastic, and then Richard held it high in the air, gave it a push off, and away it flew, whirring like a real aeroplane through the air. Sometimes it flew right down to the bottom of the garden.

The cat watched the aeroplane flying. It thought it must be some kind of toy bird. When it fell to the ground the cat went racing over to it, and pawed at it to make it fly again. But it wouldn't, of course, till Richard had wound up the elastic once more.

One day Richard flew the aeroplane when there was a very strong wind. It flew right up into the air and landed by the chimney. And there it stayed!

"Oh, dear," said Joan. "Look, Richard — it won't come back."

"It's stuck," said Richard, in dismay. "We must get a ladder."

But no ladder was long enough to reach up to the roof. Richard threw up a stick to try and dislodge the aeroplane, but Joan stopped him.

"No, don't do that — if the stick hits it, it will break a wing off the aeroplane

– and then it will never, never fly
again."

"Well, what are we to do, then –
leave it up there for ever and ever?"
said Richard, sadly. He took a step
backwards and trod on Blackie, who
had been watching all this with great
interest. Why didn't the aeroplane come
back? Why did it like being up on the
roof so much? Was there a bird's nest
up there?

Blackie squealed when Richard trod
on him. He bent down at once. "Oh,
sorry, Blackie. Did I hurt you? I didn't
see you there."

"Mee-ow," said Blackie, meaning that
it didn't matter. He strolled up to a tree
and sharpened his claws. Then up the
tree he went in a bound, and on to the
garage roof. He stopped to give himself
a little wash, while he thought of what
to do next.

Then he leapt up to the next roof,
which led to the chimneys. Joan and
Richard saw him.

"Look," said Joan. "Blackie's on the roof. I do hope he doesn't fall. I don't believe he's ever been on a roof before."

Blackie hadn't. He walked very carefully indeed. He climbed up the tiles to the chimney near to where the aeroplane rested. He came to it and sniffed at it.

"Blackie!" yelled Richard. "Blackie, be a clever cat – scrape at our aeroplane and get it down for us."

Blackie took no notice. He sniffed round, hoping to find a bird's nest. But there was none there, of course. He patted the aeroplane carefully. It moved just a little.

Blackie patted it again. He wanted it to fly as it usually did. Why wouldn't it? The wind came along and fluttered its tail. Blackie pounced on it. Up went the front part of the aeroplane as Blackie jumped at the tail, and the cat jumped back in alarm.

He nearly rolled down the tiles, but just managed to save himself. Joan squealed. Then Richard yelled loudly and made her jump.

"Look – Blackie has managed to get our aeroplane free – the wind's got it again – it's moving, it's moving!"

So it was! It slid down the roof a little way, and Blackie gave it a push. It slid all the way down the tiles with Blackie after it, came to the gutter, fell over it – and then glided down to earth through the air! It landed just by Richard.

"Oh, good cat, Blackie!" shouted Richard, in delight. "Clever cat! You've got my aeroplane back for me! Come down and we'll give you a treat!"

Blackie came down, pleased with himself. The children ran in and took some money from their money-box. Then they went to Mummy.

"Mummy," said Richard, "you've got some tins of sardines in your cupboard. Can we buy one for Blackie? He's just been very, very kind and good."

"Yes, if you like," said Mummy. "Whatever has he done?"

"He's climbed up on the roof, gone to the chimney, and set my aeroplane free for me," said Richard. "I really do think he deserves a treat."

Well, Blackie certainly enjoyed the sardines. He spent a whole hour afterwards washing himself. He wouldn't mind getting a dozen aeroplanes off the roof if he could have sardines as a reward!

And when the other cats smelt the sardine smell on him, and came round for a sniff, Blackie told them how he got such a treat – and, would you believe it, every time Joan and Richard fly that aeroplane now, at least half a dozen cats climb up to the roof and wait – just in *case* it gets stuck by the chimncy again.

"I only hope it doesn't," says Richard, each time. "There wouldn't be much left of it if *all* those cats pounce on it to set it free!"

He needn't worry. Blackie will get there first!

The goat, the duck, the goose and the cock

O nce upon a time there was a cock who was very tired of living with the hens in his yard, so he made up his mind to run away and find other friends. He set off one morning at dawn, and it wasn't long before he met a fine fat goose, walking along the lane.

"Good morning, Goose," said the cock. "Where are you off to?"

"I have lost my mistress, the goose-girl," said the goose. "I am seeking another mistress now."

"Come with me," said the cock, ruffling out his beautiful tail-feathers. "I am going to see the world."

So the goose and the cock walked on together. Presently they came to a little white duck waddling along as fast as her two unsteady legs would carry her.

"Good morning, Duck," said the cock. "Where are you off to?"

"I have heard bad news this morning," said the duck. "The red hen told me that my master was going to kill me for his supper. So I ran away, but I don't know where to go to."

"Come with us," said the cock, standing on his toes, and looking very grand. "We are going to see the world."

So the duck went with the goose and the cock, and they all walked down the lane together till they came to the common.

On the common was a billy-goat, and he had slipped the rope that tied him to his post, and was gambolling about free.

"Good morning," said the cock. "What are you going to do?"

"I don't know," said the goat, joyously. "I am free for the first time in my life – but I don't know where to go."

"Come with us," said the cock, making the red comb on his head stand up very high. "We are going to see the world."

So the goat went with the goose, the duck and the cock, and they all walked over the common together.

"What shall we do?" asked the goat.

"Shall we go to the town of Nottingham and stand by the roadside to beg?" said the cock. "I have a fine voice and I could sing for pennies."

"I could take round the hat," said the duck.

"I could clap my wings in time to your song," said the goose.

"And I could butt anyone who wouldn't give us a penny," said the goat.

So off they set for the town of Nottingham. When they got there it was market day and there were many people about. The four animals stood by

the side of the road, and the cock began to sing:

"Cock-a-doodle-doo,
My baby's lost her shoe,
It had a button blue,
What shall Baby do?"

The goose beat time with her wings, and the duck took round a hat for pennies. The goat stood by ready to butt anyone who would not give them anything.

But before the cock had quite finished his song a burly farmer came up.

"What's all this?" he cried. "Here are four creatures escaped from their pens. Catch them!"

Without waiting a moment the four animals ran away. Through the streets of Nottingham they went and found themselves on the hill outside the town.

"We were nearly caught!" said the goat. "We must not go near a town again. Whatever shall we do?"

"We had better find a cave to live in," said the cock. "See, there is one half-way up the hillside."

"A witch lives there with her ugly daughter," said the duck.

"We will go and ask her if there is another cave near by," said the goose. So off they all went. But when they got to the cave it was empty. No one was there. But there was a cupboard full of good things, and the hungry creatures had a good meal. Then they settled down to sleep.

Now that night the old witch and her daughter returned to the cave. They were a wicked couple, and the people of Nottingham had long tried to get rid of them. The witch stepped into the cave first, and lighted a candle – and the first thing she saw was the table, spread with the remains of the animals' meal.

"Someone has been here!" she cried, and stamped her foot. She and her daughter ran out of the cave and went to a nearby tree to think what they should do. They were afraid that an enemy was in the cave.

"Daughter, you creep back and find out," said the witch. "I will prepare a spell so that if any man or woman is in the cave they cannot harm you. Go."

Now when the witch had shouted and stamped her foot, the four animals had awakened in a fright. The goat was lying near the entrance of the cave, the goose was by the cupboard, the duck was under the table, and the cock was on the back of a chair. They waited to see if anything further would happen – and they heard the witch's daughter coming back.

"It's my mistress!" thought the goat.

"It's my master!" thought the duck.

"It's my mistress!" thought the cock.

"It's the goose-girl!" thought the goose. And all of them were frightened.

The witch's daughter came creeping in. She heard nothing at all. She went to the table and trod on one of the duck's feet underneath.

"Quack-quack, quack-quack-quack!" squawked the duck in pain, and dug his beak into the girl's leg. In a great fright she stumbled towards the cupboard and fell over the goose.

"Ss-ss-ss-ss-sss!" hissed the goose, and struck the witch's daughter with its great wings. Then it began to cackle loudly in fright. The girl was afraid and sat down in a chair trembling. But when she leaned back in the darkness she almost pushed the cock off the back of the chair, and he dug his claws into her hair in terror, crying "Cock-a-doodle-doo! Cock-a-doodle-doo!"

The witch's daughter could not bear it any longer. She fled to the entrance of the cave and fell right over the goat. He butted her so fiercely that she was sent rolling over and over down the hillside and only came to rest under the tree beside the witch.

"What is the matter?" cried the witch. "Didn't my spell work?"

"Oh Mother, oh Mother," said the

daughter, weeping. "The cave is full of powerful wizards. When I went in there was one under the table that cried 'Go back, go back!' And then he stuck a knife into my leg. By the cupboard is a snake that hissed at me in a dreadful manner, and then struck at me with its head. On the back of a chair sits another wizard who cried, 'What a rogue are you! What a rogue are you!' and then nearly pulled my hair out of my head. But worst of all is a giant wizard lying near the entrance. He flung me down the hillside, and here I am."

"What a dreadful thing!" said the witch, trembling. "Our sins have found us out. We must stay here no longer. Come, let us away before dawn."

They hurried off and no one ever heard of them again. As for the four animals, they soon fell asleep and slept peacefully till morning. When they awoke they looked round the cave and were pleased.

"We will live here together," said the cock. "No one will disturb us, for they think that this is a witch's home. We shall be happy here."

They settled down in peace together, and as far as I know, there they may be living still!

Mary Brown and Mary Contrary

Mary was out for a walk. She took
with her Josephine, her biggest
doll, and wheeled her in her pram. It
was a lovely day, and the sun shone
brightly.

Mary went a long way. She walked
down the little green path in Bluebell
Wood to get out of the hot sun – but
dear me, when she turned back, she
found that she had lost her way!

Somehow or other she must have
taken the wrong path – and now she
didn't know how to get back. She was
most upset.

"Never mind," she said to herself. "I

shall soon meet someone, and then I can ask them the way to my home."

In a few minutes she *did* meet someone. It was a little fat man in a green tunic. He was hurrying along with a white hen under his arm. Mary called to him.

"Please," she said, "I've lost my way. Can you tell me how to get home?"

"What is your name?" asked the fat man.

"I'm Mary," said the little girl. "And this is Josephine, one of my dolls."

"How do you do, Mary, how do you do, Josephine?" said the little man, raising his pointed cap, politely. "Yes, certainly I can show you your way home. Come with me."

Mary followed him through the wood, pushing Josephine before her in her pram. She walked down the narrow green path – and at last, to her great surprise, she came out into a little village.

What a strange village! The cottages

were very tiny indeed, and at the doors and in the gardens stood children dressed in strange suits and dresses. They looked just as if they had come out of her nursery rhyme book.

"Those two might be Jack and Jill!" thought Mary, looking at a boy and girl who stood holding a pail between them. "And that boy singing all by himself

there is just like Tommy Tucker. Look at that tiny girl sitting on a stool too – she's just like Miss Muffet eating her curds and whey!"

"We're nearly there," said the little man.

"I don't seem to know this way home," Mary said.

"Don't you?" asked the fat man in surprise, and his hen clucked loudly under his arm, as if she too was surprised. "Well – here you are. There's your cottage, look!"

Mary looked. They had stopped just outside a trim little cottage, whose walls were painted white. At the windows hung pretty curtains, and the door was painted bright yellow. It was a dear little cottage.

"But that isn't my home!" said Mary. "You've made a mistake!"

"Well, didn't you say that you were Mary?" asked the little man, in astonishment. "This is Mary's cottage. Look, there's the name on the gate."

Mary looked. Sure enough on the gate the words 'MARY'S COTTAGE' were painted.

"And look – there are your cockle shells making a nice border to your flower-beds," said the little man, pointing. "And there are your pretty Canterbury Bells, all flowering nicely in the sunshine."

Mary stared at the cottage garden. She saw that each flower-bed was neatly edged with cockle-shells, and that wonderful Canterbury Bells flowered everywhere, their blossoms just like silver bells, instead of being blue or white.

"And there are your pretty maids all in a row!" said the little man, waving his hand to where a row of pretty dolls sat on the grass. "Look, your doll wants to join them."

To Mary's great astonishment she saw her doll Josephine getting out of the pram! Josephine walked through the garden gate and sat herself down in the row of dolls, who seemed very pleased to see her. Then the wind blew and all the Canterbury Bells began to ring – tinkle – tinkle – tinkle!

Mary was too surprised to speak. She couldn't understand it at all – and yet she felt she had seen all this before somewhere – was it in a book?

"*Isn't* this your home?" asked the little man, looking puzzled. "Your name is Mary, Mary, Quite Contrary, isn't it?"

"No, it isn't!" cried Mary, seeing where he had made his mistake. "I'm just Mary Brown! You thought I was some other Mary – the Mary of the nursery rhyme. *You* know, Mary, Mary, Quite Contrary, How does your garden grow? With silver bells and cockle-shells, And pretty maids all in a row!"

"Well, of *course* I thought you were!" said the little man. "I'm so sorry. I've brought you ever so far out of your way."

Just then the door of the cottage opened and a little girl about Mary's age came out. She was a pretty little girl with long curly hair, and she had a big sun-bonnet on her head. Her dress reached right to her shoes and her little feet twinkled in and out as she walked.

"I say, Mary, Quite Contrary!" called the little man. "I've made a dreadful mistake. This little girl's name is Mary, and I've brought her to your cottage thinking she lived here – and she doesn't!"

"Dear me," said Mary Contrary, in a soft little voice. "What a pity! Never mind – she had better come in and rest a little while. She shall have dinner with me, and then I'll see that she gets home all right."

Mary was delighted. She liked Mary Contrary very much indeed. It would be lovely to have dinner with her. She said goodbye to the little man who had made the mistake, and he hurried off down the street, with the hen under his arm clucking loudly.

Mary walked into the garden, and the other Mary took her into her spick-and-span cottage. It was so pretty inside – very small, like a doll's house – but quite big enough for the two children.

"It's so hot that I thought of having ice-cream pudding and ginger-beer for dinner today," said Mary Contrary, "I hope that will suit you all right, Mary."

"Oh yes!" said Mary, delighted. "I think that's the nicest dinner I ever heard of!"

Mary Contrary bustled about getting the table laid and Mary Brown helped her. Then they sat down to the largest ice-cream pudding Mary had ever seen – and do you know, they finished it between them! Then they had a bottle of ginger-beer each. It was really lovely.

"This is the village of Nursery Rhyme," said Mary Contrary. "Tom the Piper's Son lives over there – he's a very naughty boy. I don't have much to do with *him*! Next door lives Jack Horner, but he has a very good opinion of himself – he's always saying that he is a very good boy!"

"Yes, I know all about him," said Mary Brown. "Does Humpty-Dumpty live here too?"

"Yes," said Mary Contrary. "But, you know, he's very silly. He's been warned heaps of times not to sit on walls – but he always will. Then he falls off, and as he is a great big egg, he breaks, and there's such a mess to clear up. All the King's horses and all the King's men can't mend him. But he's all right again by the morning – and off he goes to sit on the wall once more!"

"I wish I could see him," said Mary, excited. "This is a lovely place, I think. Does Polly Flinders live here too?"

"Yes, but she's a dirty little girl," said Mary Contrary, wrinkling up her nose in disgust. "She sits among the cinders and spoils all her nice new clothes. There is the Black Sheep here too. He doesn't belong to Bo Peep, though – all *her* sheep are white. She's a silly girl, she's always losing them."

"But they come home all right, don't they?" asked Mary, anxiously.

"Oh yes, and bring their tails behind them," answered Mary Contrary. "Will you have some more ginger-beer? No? Well, now, what about getting you home? I'll walk part of the way with you – and perhaps you wouldn't mind if I gave one of my pretty maids – my dolls, you know – a ride in Josephine's pram for a treat?"

"Of course!" said Mary, getting up and smiling. "I know Josephine would love to have someone in the pram with her."

So Mary Contrary tucked up Esmeralda, her best pretty maid, into the pram beside Josephine, and the two dolls were very happy to be with one another. Mary loved to see her own doll smiling so cheerfully.

Off the two little girls went. Mary looked excitedly at all the little houses she passed. A little girl with a red cloak and hood stood at the door of one and Mary felt sure she was Red Riding Hood. She saw Johnny Thin who put the cat in the well, and Johnny Stout, who pulled him out. She waved to the Old Woman who lived in a shoe, and wished she could go nearer to the funny old house in the shape of a shoe and look at it. But she was afraid that the Old Woman might think she was one of her many children, and put her to bed.

At last they left the strange village behind and went into the wood. It wasn't very long before they were on the right path to Mary's home.

"Well, you know the way now," said Mary Contrary kissing Mary Brown. "Do come and see me again, won't you? And be sure to bring Josephine with you."

She took Esmeralda out of the pram, kissed Josephine goodbye, and stood waving to Mary as she went along the green path. Mary hurried along, anxious to tell her mother all her adventures.

Mother *was* surprised! She couldn't believe her ears!

"Well, you shall come with me next time I go to see Mary Contrary," promised Mary Brown. "I know you'll love to see everybody!"

So her mother is going with her tomorrow. I *do* hope they find the right path, don't you?

Conceited Clara

C lara was a doll — and goodness, what a marvellous doll she was! She wore a blue silk dress, a wonderful coat to match, blue shoes and socks, and a hat that was so full of flowers it looked like a little garden.

It was the hat that everyone admired so much. There were daisies, buttercups, cornflowers, poppies and grass round the hat, and it suited Clara perfectly. She knew this, so she always wore her hat, even when she played games with the toys.

"You are vain, Clara!" said the teddy bear teasingly.

That made Clara go red. She *was* vain, and she knew she was pretty.

She knew that her clothes were lovely. She knew that her flowery hat was the prettiest one the toys had ever seen, and that it made her look really sweet.

"I'm not vain!" said Clara. "Not a bit!"

"You are! You're conceited and stuck-up," said the teddy bear, who always said what he thought. "You even wear

your hat when you play with us. And if we play a bit roughly you turn up your nose and say, 'Oh, please! You'll tear my pretty frock!' Pooh! Conceited Clara!"

Clara was angry. She glared at the bear and then she walked straight up to him. She took hold of his pink bow and tugged at it. It came undone, and Clara pulled it off. And then she tore the ribbon in half. Wasn't she naughty?

"Oh! You horrid doll! Look what you've done! You've torn my ribbon and now I can't tie it round my neck, and I shall show where my head is sewn on to my body," wept the bear.

"Serves you right," said Clara, and she walked off.

Well, after that the toys wouldn't have anything to do with Clara. They wouldn't play with her. They wouldn't talk to her. They wouldn't even speak when she called to them. So Clara was cross and unhappy.

One night, when the children were asleep and the toys came alive to play, Clara took her beautiful flowery hat and hung it up in the dolls' house. She thought perhaps the toys might play with her if she didn't wear her hat. She fluffed out her curly hair and gazed at the teddy bear.

"Ho!" said the bear. "Now you want to show off your curly hair, I suppose! Well, go and show it somewhere else! *We* don't want to see it, Conceited Clara!"

So that wasn't any use. Clara went to a corner and sulked. She was very angry. How dare the toys take no notice of her, the prettiest doll in the whole nursery!

Then the toys planned a party. It was the birthday of the clockwork mouse, and everyone loved him because he was such a dear. So they thought they would have a party for him and games, and give him a lovely time.

But they didn't ask Clara. The teddy

cooked some exciting cakes and biscuits on the stove in the dolls' house, and cut up a rosy apple into slices. The toys set out the chairs round the little wooden table and put the dishes and plates ready.

Everything looked so nice. "It's a pity that we can't put a vase of flowers in the middle of the table," said the teddy bear. "I always think flowers look so sweet at a party. Come along, everyone – we'll just go and tidy ourselves up and then the party can begin."

They all went to find the brush and comb in the toy-cupboard. Clara peeped from her corner and thought that the birthday-table looked lovely with its cakes and biscuits and apple-slices.

"I do wish I had something to give the clockwork mouse," thought Clara. "I do love him. He's such a dear. But I expect he would throw it back at me if I had anything to give. The toys are all so horrid to me now."

And then Clara suddenly had a

marvellous idea. What about her flowery hat? Couldn't she take the flowers off that beautiful hat and put them into a vase for the middle of the birthday-table? They would look really lovely.

She rushed to get her hat. She tore the flowers from it. She found a dear little vase, and began to put them in – buttercups, daisies, cornflowers, poppies and grass. You can't think how sweet they looked.

Clara popped the vase of flowers in the middle of the table and went back to her corner. She looked at her hat rather sadly. It looked very odd without its flowers. She would look funny if she wore it any more.

The toys ran to the birthday-table to begin the party – and how they stared when they saw the lovely flowers in the middle of the table!

"Where did they come from?" cried the teddy bear in astonishment.

"Oh, what a lovely surprise for me!"

cried the clockwork mouse. And then he guessed who had put the flowers there for him.

"It's Clara! They are the flowers out of her hat!" he squeaked. "Oh, Clara, thank you! Do, do come to my party!"

"Yes, do come!" cried all the toys. And the bear ran and took her hand.

"If you can give up the flowers you were so proud of, you can't be so horrid after all!" he cried. "Come along, Clara, and join the party."

So Clara went, and everyone was so nice to her that she was quite happy again. Sometimes she wears her hat without the flowers, and do you know what the toys say? They say, "Why, Clara, you look just as nice without the flowers – you really do!"

And so she does!

Mother Hubbard's honey

Mother Hubbard kept bees, and they made lovely golden honey for her. Mother Hubbard took it from the hives and put it into jars.

Then her cupboard was full when she went to it, instead of bare. Rows upon rows of honey jars stood there, waiting to be sold.

Now little Pixie Peep-About lived next door to Mother Hubbard, and he loved honey. But he wasn't a very good or very helpful pixie, so Mother Hubbard didn't give him any honey. She sold most of it, gave some to her friends, and kept six pots for herself.

Pixie Peep-About was cross because she never gave him any honey. "And I

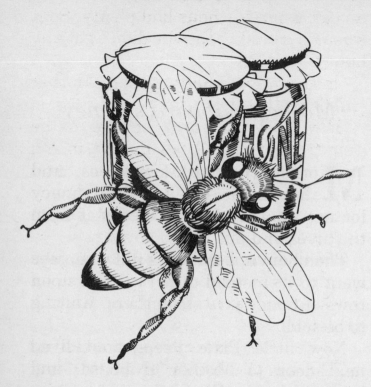

live next door, too!" he said to himself.
"She might have given me just a taste.
She knows I love honey."

But Peep-About never gave Mother
Hubbard any of his gooseberries when

they were ripe. And he didn't offer her an egg when his hens laid plenty. So it wasn't surprising that he didn't get any honey.

One summer he watched Mother Hubbard's bees.

"How busy they are!" he said, as he peeped over the wall. "In and out, in and out of those hives all the day long. And what is more, a lot of those bees come into *my* garden and take the honey from *my* flowers!"

It was quite true. They did. But bees go anywhere and everywhere, so of course they went into Peep-About's garden too.

"Some of that honey they are storing in Mother Hubbard's hives is mine, taken from my flowers," thought Peep-About. "So Mother Hubbard ought to give me plenty!"

He told Mother Hubbard this, but she laughed. "Honey is free in the flowers!" she said. "Don't be silly, Peep-About."

Now, one day Mother Hubbard went

to take the honeycombs from her hives. They were beautiful combs, full of golden honey. She meant to separate the honey from the combs, and store it in her jars. Peep-About knew she was going to do that. She did it every year.

"Now she'll have jars upon jars of honey, and she won't give me a single one," thought the pixie. "It's too bad. I haven't tasted honey for months, and I should love some on bread and butter."

Mother Hubbard poured the honey into her jars. She handed one to old Mister Potter, at the bottom of the garden. He was a kind old fellow, and always gave Mother Hubbard tomatoes when he had some to spare. He was delighted.

"Look at that now!" said Peep-About to himself. "Not a drop for me! Mean old thing! My, what delicious honey it looked!"

The next day Mother Hubbard

dressed herself up in her best coat and hat, and set out to catch the bus, with three pots of honey in her basket. Peep-About met her as she went to the bus.

"Where are you going?" asked Peep-About.

"To see my sister, Dame Blue-Bonnet," said Mother Hubbard. "I'll be gone all day, so if you see the milkman, Peep-About, tell him to leave me a pint of milk."

"Gone all day!" thought Peep-About. "Well, what about me getting in at the kitchen window, going to that cupboard, and helping myself to a few spoonfuls of honey!"

So, when Mother Hubbard had safely got on the bus, Peep-About crept in at her kitchen window and went to the cupboard. It wasn't locked. He opened it, and saw row upon row of jars of honey. Oh, what a lovely sight!

He was small and the cupboard was high. He tried to scramble up to one of the shelves, and he upset a jar of honey. Down it went, and poured all over him!

"Gracious!" said Peep-About in alarm. "It's all over me! How lovely it tastes!"

He thought he had better go into his own home, scrape the honey off himself, and eat it that way. So out of the window he went.

But the garden was full of Mother Hubbard's bees, and they smelt the honey on Peep-About at once.

"Zzzzzz! Honey! ZZZZZZZ! Honey!" they buzzed to one another, and flew round Peep-About. They tried to settle on the honey that was running down his head and neck.

"Go away! Go away! Stop buzzing round me!" he cried. But no matter how he waved them away, they came back again.

And now Peep-About had a terrible time, for wherever he went the bees went too. They followed him into his kitchen. They stung him when he flapped them away. They followed him out into the garden again. They followed him into the street. They wouldn't leave Peep-About alone for one minute.

He couldn't sit down and have his dinner. He had to go without his tea. He ran here and he ran there, but always the bees flew with him.

He had their honey on him, and they wanted it.

More and more bees came to join in the fun. At last Peep-About saw Mother Hubbard walking up her front path and he ran to her. She was astonished to see her bees round him in a big buzzing cloud.

"Take them away! Make them go to their hive!" wept Peep-About.

Mother Hubbard touched him and found he was sticky with honey. Then she knew what had happened.

"You went to steal some of my honey," she said, sternly. "You're a bad pixie. You can keep the honey – and the bees too! I shan't call them off!"

So, until the bees went to bed in their hive that night, poor Peep-About had to put up with them. He ran for miles trying to get rid of them, but he couldn't. They could fly faster than he could run!

At last the bees went to bed.

Peep-About stripped off his sticky suit and washed it. He got himself a meal. He cried all the time. "I shall never like honey again," he wept. "Never, never, never!"

Mother Hubbard was sorry the next day that she hadn't helped poor Peep-About, even though he had been a bad little pixie. So she sent him a tiny jar of honey all for himself.

But wasn't it a pity – he couldn't eat it! He didn't like honey any more. He couldn't bear to look at it.

"It serves me right!" he said. "When I couldn't have it, I loved it, and tried to take it. Now, here I've got a jar, and I can't bear to eat it. It's a good punishment for me, it really is!"

She was always at the bottom

Janie did her very best at school, but no matter how she tried, she always was at the bottom of her class. Wasn't it a pity?

She wasn't any good at sums, and her writing was rather like spiders'

legs running over the page. She found it very difficult to read, and she couldn't sing in tune.

But Mummy didn't really mind. "I know you do your best, darling," she often said to Janie. "That's all that matters."

Janie didn't worry for herself – she was only sorry because, when the prize-giving day came, she never had a prize and couldn't make her mother proud of her. She saw all the other children proudly going up to the platform to get prizes for sums, writing, and reading, but Janie had to sit still in her seat, for there was never a prize for her.

Once her mummy found her crying about it, and she put her arm round her to comfort her.

"Janie, you may not be the cleverest girl in the school, you may not be the hardest-working girl – but there is something you *can* be, if you try."

"What's that, Mummy?" asked Janie, wiping her eyes.

"You can be the kindest girl!" said Mummy. "What about trying that, Janie? I shall be very proud of you, then. A great many boys and girls can be clever – but it isn't everyone that is kind."

Well, Janie thought she would try. So she began. She sharpened Donald's pencils for him. She broke her rubber in half and gave a piece to Gladys when she had lost hers. She shared her biscuits with George when he had forgotten his one morning.

She brought Miss Brown some flowers from her own little garden at home. She offered to take home the caterpillars each weekend to look after them for the class – and she looked after them well, too.

"Really, Janie, you're a very helpful girl," Miss Brown said. "You were bottom of the class again this week, but for helpfulness I really think you are at the top!"

Janie was pleased! She found that

the other children liked her more and more, because she was always kind and generous to them. If the little ones fell down and hurt their knees, it was always Janie they went to, to be bandaged. If anybody trapped their fingers in desks or doors, they would run to Janie at once.

Soon the end of the term came along as usual. The children began to talk about exams and marks and prizes.

"I shall be top in maths!" said George proudly. "I was last year, too."

"And I'm sure I shall get the writing prize," said Ellen. "I hope it's a book. I love reading."

"Miss Brown says if I work as hard as I have been doing all the term I shall have the reading prize," said Donald, who was a wonderful reader.

Janie listened and said nothing. There wasn't anything she could get a prize for, she knew. The children looked at her. Last year they had laughed at Janie because she was the dunce, and didn't get any prizes at all. But this year they didn't laugh.

"You know, I do so like Janie," said Ellen to Donald. "I'm sorry she won't get a prize. It must be horrid for her to sit beside her mother whilst we go up and collect our prizes. Other people who don't get prizes this year probably got them last year – but Janie never gets one any year!"

Well, all the children got together in a corner of the playground one morning and had a talk about Janie. Janie couldn't imagine what they were talking about! They wouldn't let her come near them, and she felt rather hurt.

"Oh dear! Why are they leaving me out?" she thought. "This is horrid!"

But the children were not really being horrid. They were planning a nice surprise for Janie!

"Do let's all bring a penny or two and ask Miss Brown to buy a prize for Janie!" they were saying.

"But whatever shall we give her a prize for?" wondered Alice. "She isn't really good at anything, not even games or needlework."

"Well, she's jolly good at being kind," said George. "Let's say it's a prize for kindness."

Well, after they had planned this, they went to Miss Brown. Still they wouldn't let Janie into their secret and the little girl went home in tears. She couldn't understand why she was being left out of the children's secrets so suddenly.

Miss Brown thought it was a splendid idea. She smiled at the children. "Bring your pennies," she said, "and I will count them and see what we can buy."

So, very secretly, each child brought five pence or ten pence, and some even brought twenty pence. They gave the money to Miss Brown and she counted it all up.

"There is quite a lot," she said. "One pound and twenty-five pence! What shall we buy for Janie's prize?"

"She won't want a book," said Donald. "She doesn't read well enough, and she's not fond of games like snap or ludo. But, Miss Brown, she does love dolls."

"Well, what about a doll?" said Miss Brown. "Alice, you come with me this afternoon and look in the toyshop to see what sort of dolls they have."

So Alice and Miss Brown looked in the toyshop that afternoon – and there they saw a lovely baby doll, dressed in a woolly dress and jacket, smiling at them.

"That's just what Janie would like!" cried Alice. "But, oh dear – it's one pound and seventy-five pence! I can give ten pence more of my money towards the price, Miss Brown, but that's all I've got."

"Well, I will give the extra forty pence," said Miss Brown. "So the prize will be from me, too. Come along into the shop and we'll buy the doll."

In they went – and the baby doll was

soon packed into a long box with tissue-paper round her face. Alice proudly carried the box back to school, and that afternoon she showed the children Janie's prize. Even the boys liked the doll.

"It looks such a smiley doll," said George.

Janie had been sent home first by Miss Brown. She wondered why. Really, everyone seemed to be keeping her out of their secrets lately. It was too bad!

"Mummy, it's the prize-giving day tomorrow," she told her mother when the day came near. "You won't be very proud of me again, I'm afraid, because I'm bottom in all the exams. But I've got to go tomorrow afternoon. Would you like to come, or do you think it will be a waste of time for you when you have a little girl who never wins anything?"

"Of course I'll come," said Mummy at once. "There is going to be singing and reciting too, isn't there, Janie? I'd love to hear that."

"Yes, but I'm not in anything much," said Janie sadly. "And lately the children have been having secrets and not telling me, Mummy. So it hasn't been much good me trying to be kind, as you said."

"It's always worthwhile being kind," said Mummy. "Don't stop, Janie. Just go on, please."

Well, the prize-giving afternoon came at last. The children sang and recited. The headmistress made a speech. Miss Brown said a few words too. All the parents clapped and cheered.

Then the prizes were given out. One by one the children went up to the platform and took their books, games, and toys. They were so proud. Their mothers clapped them loudly, feeling very pleased indeed. Janie's mother clapped all the other children too, and so did Janie.

And then came the surprise of the afternoon. Miss Brown got up and went to the front, when only one prize remained to be given.

"And now," she said, "I have a very special prize, given for a very special thing. This prize is given by all the children and by me, too – not for any lessons or games or handiwork – but for kindness. Janie White, you may not be top of lessons – but you *are* top in kindness! Please come up and get your prize!"

Janie simply couldn't believe her ears! Why, she had won a prize – a real prize for herself, at last! And a prize for kindness, too! The little girl went as red as a beetroot, and stood up to go to the platform. Her mother was so surprised and delighted that she almost forgot to clap Janie!

And you should have heard the clapping and cheering when Janie went up to get her prize! It was far louder and much longer than it had been for anyone else.

"Three cheers for our Janie!" yelled Donald. "Hip, hip, hurrah!"

Miss Brown patted Janie on the shoulder. The headmistress smiled at her. Janie took her big box and walked back to her mother, prouder than she had ever been in her life. When she undid the box and saw the doll smiling up at her, she was so pleased that she danced round her seat in joy.

She took the doll home. She got ready a cot for it. She bathed it and put a night-dress on its fat little body. She was very happy indeed.

"Janie," said her mother, "I would far rather you had a prize for kindness than for any lesson. I am VERY proud of you."

"I know now why the children were having secrets," said Janie. "They were planning my prize! Oh, Mummy, let's give a party for my new doll and ask all the children to it. Wouldn't it be fun?"

Well, the party is tomorrow, and the doll has a new frock for it. All the children are going – I expect you'd like to go too, if you could, wouldn't you?

The empty dolls' house

Sally had a lovely little dolls' house on Christmas Day. She looked at it standing there at the foot of her bed. It had a little blue front door with a tiny knocker that really knocked, and it had four small windows, with tiny lace curtains at each!

"Oh, it's lovely!" said Sally. "Won't my little Belinda Jane love to live there! She is small enough to fit it properly."

But when she opened the front of the dolls' house, Sally got rather a shock. It was empty. There was no furniture at all!

She was disappointed. A dolls' house can't be played with unless it has furniture inside, and Sally badly wanted to play with it.

Also, Belinda Jane couldn't possibly live there if it was empty. She must at least have a bed to sleep in, a chair to sit on, and a table to have meals on.

She showed the house to Belinda Jane. Belinda looked sad when she saw that it was empty.

"Never mind. I'll save up my money and buy some furniture," said Sally. "Maybe I'll get some money today for a present."

But she didn't. All her aunts and

uncles gave her Christmas presents of toys and books, and nobody gave her any money at all.

It was Granny who had given her the dear little dolls' house. When she came to share Christmas dinner she spoke to Sally about the house.

"I didn't put any furniture in it, dear," she said, "because I thought you would find it more fun to buy some yourself and furnish it bit by bit."

"Yes. It *will* be fun to do that," said Sally. "Only it will take such a long time, Granny, because I spent all my money on Christmas presents, and I only get fifty pence a week, you know."

When Sally got her first fifty pence she went to the toyshop and looked at the dolls' furniture there. She saw a cardboard box, and in it was a dear little bed that would just fit Belinda Jane, two chairs, a table and a wardrobe! Think of that!

But, oh dear, it cost three pounds, and

there was nothing at all that fifty pence would buy! Sally ran home almost in tears!

"Now don't be a baby," said Mummy. "Everything comes to those who wait patiently. Don't get cross and upset if you can't have what you want. It will come!"

Sally was not a very patient person, and she hated waiting for things she badly wanted. But she always believed what Mummy said, so she went up to the playroom and told Belinda Jane they must both be patient, and maybe they would get the furniture somehow in the end.

Sally was excited next day, because she was going to a party – and there was to be a Christmas tree. It was sure to be a nice big one, with a present for everyone. And there would be games and balloons and crackers and ice-creams. Lovely!

She went to the party in her best blue dress. "Hallo, Sally!" cried Eileen, dancing up to her. "There's going to be a prize for every game, did you know? And it's to be money! I do hope I win a prize, because it's Mummy's birthday next week, and I want to buy her some flowers."

Sally was pleased to hear about the prizes, too. If only she could win some of the money! She would be able to buy some furniture for Belinda Jane.

They played musical chairs – but Sally didn't win because a rough little boy pushed her out of her chair, and she didn't like to push back.

They played hunt the thimble, but somehow Sally never could see the thimble first! And when they played spin the tray she couldn't get there before the little spinning tray had fallen over flat! So she didn't win any prizes at all.

"Now, I mustn't get cross or upset," she said to herself. "I mustn't. I must be patient. But I've missed my chance.

What a pity!"

After tea the children were taken into another room — and there was the Christmas tree, reaching up to the ceiling, hung with presents from top to bottom.

Just about the middle of the tree there hung a cardboard box — the cardboard box of furniture that Sally had seen in the toyshop! Her heart jumped for joy. Now surely her patience would have its reward — surely she would get that lovely box of dolls' furniture!

She could hardly wait for the presents to be given out. She had good manners, so she didn't like to ask for the box of furniture. She just stood near by, hoping it would be hers.

But to her very great disappointment, it wasn't given to her! She was handed a box with tiny cars in it instead. Sally could have cried! She said, "Thank you," and went to a corner, trying not to feel upset.

"I wanted to win a prize and I didn't. And I wanted to have the furniture off the tree and I didn't," she thought. "What's the good of being patient? I don't get what I want, however good and patient I am. I feel like shouting and stamping!"

But she didn't shout or stamp, of course, because she knew better. She just sat and looked at the little cars, and didn't like them a bit.

A small girl called Fanny came up to her. She held the box of furniture in her hand. She sat down beside Sally and looked at the tiny cars.

"Oh, aren't they lovely?" she said. "I do like them so much. I got this dolls' furniture, look. Isn't it silly?"

"Well, I think it's lovely," said Sally. "How *can* you think it's silly?"

"It's silly for me, because I haven't got a dolls' house," said Fanny. "But I *have* got a toy garage! I had it for Christmas. It's only got one car in, and I do want some more. That's why I like your present and hate mine!"

"Well, *I* had a dolls' house for Christmas without any furniture – and I haven't got a garage!" said Sally, her face very bright. "Can't you give me the furniture and I'll give you the cars? We could ask Eileen's mother, and see if she minds. It was she who bought all the presents for us."

They ran to Eileen's mother, and told her. She smiled at them. "Of course, change your presents if you want to," she said. "I think it would be most sensible of you. I should have given *you* the furniture, Sally, and *you* the cars, Fanny, if I'd known about the dolls' house and the garage."

The little girls were so pleased. Fanny took her cars home to her toy garage and Sally raced home with her dolls' furniture. It went into the dolls' house and looked most beautiful!

"There you are, Belinda Jane," said Sally to her smallest doll. "Now you can move in. You've got a bed to sleep in,

chairs to sit on, a wardrobe for your clothes and a table to have meals on. And I'll buy you a little cooker as soon as ever I can."

Belinda Jane was pleased. She looked sweet sitting on one of the chairs, and even sweeter tucked up in the little bed.

Mummy came to look. Sally gave her a hug. "Mummy, you were right about waiting patiently. I kept *on* being disappointed, but I wouldn't get cross or upset – and then suddenly the furniture just came to me. Wasn't it lucky?"

"It was," said Mummy. "Now, tomorrow I'll give you some old bits-and-pieces and you can make carpets for Belinda Jane. She will like that."

You should see Sally's dolls' house now. She saved up her money and bought a little lamp, a cooker, another bed, a cupboard for the kitchen, two more chairs and a dressing table. I really wouldn't mind living in that dolls' house myself!

You can't trick Brer Rabbit

N ow once it happened that Brer
Rabbit went along the lane near
Brer Fox's house, and saw Brer Fox
filling a sack. Brer Rabbit stopped at
once.

"Heyo, Brer Fox!" he called. "What's
that you're collecting? Ha! Ripe apples!
Juicy windfalls! My, that tree is loaded,
isn't it?"

"It is," said Brer Fox. "But not one
apple do you get, Brer Rabbit! Not one.
You're no friend of mine, and I'm giving
you no apples!"

Brer Rabbit sat on the wall and
watched, humming a jolly little tune.
Brer Fox didn't like being watched.
What trick was Brer Rabbit up to now?

"If you think you're going to pick up apples after I'm gone, you're wrong," he said. "I'm picking up every single one. And there's no wind, so no more will fall down. You can sit on that wall as long as you choose, you won't get a single apple."

"Who wants rotten apples?" said Brer Rabbit. "Only miserly foxes! You can keep them, Brer Fox. I like my apples off the tree, sound and ripe."

Brer Fox grinned. "Ho! Well, you're welcome to sit there and *look* at my apples," he said. "But the tree is too high for you to climb, Brer Rabbit — and you're no good at climbing, anyway. Good day to you. I'm off to make an apple pie for dinner!"

He went off with his sack. Brer Rabbit waited till he had gone into his house, and then he leapt off the wall and went round to Brer Fox's shed.

Brer Fox looked out of the window. He couldn't see Brer Rabbit on the wall, and he thought he had gone home. He grinned. Aha! That was the way to talk to that cheeky rascal!

But Brer Rabbit was very busy in the shed. He was looking for Brer Fox's ladder. Ah – there it was. He could get it out and take it to the apple tree quite easily without being seen. Brer Fox would be busy peeling his apples for a pie. He would never guess what Brer Rabbit was up to!

Brer Rabbit put the ladder over his shoulder, crept round the shed and went out the back way. He was soon in the field outside Brer Fox's garden, where the big apple tree stood.

"Up you go!" said Brer Rabbit to the ladder, and put it against the tree. "And up I go, too!"

He was soon in the tree, filling his pocket with the apples. Why should Brer Fox think that was *his* tree? It wasn't even in his garden! It belonged to anybody – and everyone should have a share of the apples.

"I'm having *my* share, anyway!" said Brer Rabbit, gleefully, as he stuffed his big pockets full. He bit into a rosy apple. It was delicious! He sat up there enjoying himself, eating three apples one after another.

Now it happened that Brer Fox wanted something out of his shed, and he went to get it. He found the door open – and the ladder gone!

"That's Brer Rabbit! He's got my ladder – and he's up that tree taking the apples – the good, ripe ones I'm saving to sell at the market!" said Brer Fox, angrily. "The rogue! The rascal! The scamp! The – the – well, I can't think of bad enough names. I'll get him! I'll teach him to take my ladder without asking, and get up that tree!"

And out of the shed went Brer Fox, grinding his big teeth, ready to eat Brer Rabbit for his dinner!

He came to the apple tree. Yes – there was his ladder. He shouted up the tree and gave Brer Rabbit such a fright that he nearly fell out.

"You up there! How dare you? I'm coming up after you, and that will be the end of you, you rascally rabbit!"

"You come on up, Brer Fox, and I'll give you one big shove, and down you'll go again!" shouted back Brer Rabbit.

Brer Fox stopped halfway up the ladder. He thought hard. Brer Rabbit *would* give him a push, there was no doubt about that – and down he would go.

Brer Fox got down the ladder again, a sudden idea making him laugh. "Stay up there all you like!" he called. "Eat apples till you look like one! I'm taking the ladder away, and I'm fetching Brer Wolf and Brer Bear. Old Brer Bear can climb up and push you down – and Brer Wolf and I will catch you. Ho, yes – we'll catch you at last. You'll taste nice with onions and carrots, Brer Rabbit, so you will!"

And with that he swung the ladder away from the tree and dropped it on the ground. Then off he went to fetch Brer Wolf and Brer Bear.

Brer Rabbit stopped eating apples. He peered down the tree. No – he really couldn't climb down it. Its trunk was too bare – he would slip and hurt himself. What was he to do then? Wait there quietly till he was caught by the others?

Brer Rabbit didn't like the look of things at all – and then he saw somebody coming by. Who was it? He peered down.

"It's Mr Benjamin Ram," he thought. "Well – maybe he'll get me out of this fix! Hey, Mr Benjamin! How do you feel today?"

"I'm suffering," said Mr Ram, looking up into the tree. "Suffering from hunger, Brer Rabbit. Not a bite have I had since yesterday. Throw me down an apple."

"One apple's no good to a hungry man!" said Brer Rabbit. "You come on up here and munch away, Mr Benjamin Ram. Why, there's a branch here so covered with apples that you could munch for a month of Sundays and you'd still find plenty!"

Mr Ram's mouth began to water. He loved apples. Good, juicy apples! But how could he get up the tree?

"I can't get up," he called. "Throw me an apple down – throw me a dozen!"

"You come on up and have a hundred or two," said Brer Rabbit, generously. "You'll find a ladder just over there, on the ground, Mr Ram. Stick it up against the tree and come and share the fruit with me. Have as much as you like! Eat all the apples on it, I don't mind!"

"That's right down generous of you, Brer Rabbit," said Mr Ram, delighted. "I'll just get the ladder."

So he got the ladder and put it against the tree. Up he went nimbly, and was soon on the branch beside Brer Rabbit. Certainly the tree was laden. Mr Ram didn't bother to fill his pockets – he just munched along a branch – munch – munch – munch. Apple after apple disappeared, and Mr Ram's beard wagged as he munched each one.

"I think I'll get down now," said Brer Rabbit, who was keeping a sharp eye out for Brer Fox and his friends. He could see them coming in the distance. "I've got enough. But you stay on up the tree, Mr Ram, and eat all you want. I'm not mean, like Brer Fox. You have all you like!"

Mr Benjamin Ram thought Brer Rabbit was the kindest fellow in the world. Munch – munch – munch. What a feast! Brer Rabbit slipped down the ladder quickly, took it away from the tree, and laid it on the ground again. Then he skipped behind a bush to see the fun, grinning all over his furry face.

Up came Brer Fox with Brer Wolf and Brer Bear. He picked up the ladder and set it against the tree. Then he called up.

"Brer Rabbit! Here comes Brer Bear. One shove from him, and you'll fall into our arms. We're waiting for you, Brer Rabbit, we're waiting!"

Mr Benjamin Ram heard all this, but as his name wasn't Brer Rabbit, he didn't answer. He went on munching. Munch – munch – munch. Brer Fox heard him and showed his teeth in a fury. "Just you wait, Brer Rabbit! Munching like that!"

Brer Bear went up the ladder. He was

very surprised to see the bearded face of Mr Ram suddenly looking down at him. Mr Ram didn't like Brer Bear.

"Get out," he said to him, and butted him hard with his horns. Brer Bear went flying out of the tree and landed on top of Brer Fox. Brer Fox felt as if a steam-roller had fallen on him, and he groaned.

"Pah!" said Brer Wolf in disgust. "Fancy you letting a little fellow like Brer Rabbit fling you out of a tree, Brer Bear. *I'll* go up and get him!"

And, before Brer Bear could get his breath to warn him, up he went into the tree. Mr Ram was waiting for him, munching all the time. Biff! BIFF! Poor Brer Wolf didn't even see what hit him, and Mr Ram butted hard. He went flying out of the tree, too, and again poor Brer Fox was flattened out as Brer Wolf landed heavily on top of him.

This was too much for Brer Rabbit. He rolled on the ground beside his bush, laughing fit to kill himself. "Ho, ho, ho!

Ha, ha, ha! Good old Mr Ram! Do it again, Benjamin, do it again. No, don't – I'll burst with laughing if you do!"

Brer Wolf, Brer Fox and Brer Bear glared at Brer Rabbit in a rage – but they couldn't chase him, they were so bumped and bruised.

"I can't run a step!" groaned Brer Fox.

But he could! Mr Ram suddenly decided that he had had enough apples, and he came down the ladder, and ran at the three of them with his horns down to butt them.

How they ran! They ran for their lives, and Mr Ram galloped after them. But he was too full of apples to catch them, and they rushed into Brer Fox's house and slammed the door in his face.

They could hear Brer Rabbit's shouts of laughter as they sank into chairs. Brer Wolf growled.

"Wait till I catch Brer Rabbit! Just wait!" he said.

Well – he's still waiting!

Brer Rabbit's
Christmas supper

One Christmas there was very little in Brer Rabbit's larder or in Brer Terrapin's either. They sat and looked at one another gloomily. What could they have for their Christmas supper?

Now just before Christmas Brer Fox called in at Brer Rabbit's. "Heyo, Brer Rabbit!" he said. "Would you like to come and share my Christmas supper with me? You come along, do! Brer Wolf's coming and Brer Bear, too. We'd love to have your company."

Brer Rabbit felt rather doubtful. "I didn't know you'd got anything in your larder," he said.

"Aha, you wait and see!" said Brer Fox. "We'll maybe have chicken stew – ah, yes, with carrots and onions and turnips – all the things you like, Brer Rabbit."

It sounded very good. But Brer Rabbit didn't trust Brer Fox. Brer Fox was a wily one. So was Brer Rabbit. He sat and wondered if he should say yes, he'd go, or no, he wouldn't be along.

"I'll come," he said at last. "And thank you kindly, Brer Fox. I'll be along in good time for supper."

Brer Fox grinned and went. Brer Rabbit hopped along to tell Brer Terrapin. "You be careful now," said Brer Terrapin. "Brer Fox doesn't go giving food away when his larder's as empty as yours is! He'll be making a meal of *you*, Brer Rabbit, that's what he'll be doing."

"Well, he won't, Brer Terrapin, he won't," said Brer Rabbit. "You and I are going to make a nice little plan, see? And we'll have a nice little dinner all to ourselves on Christmas night. You see if we don't."

Now, on Christmas night Brer Rabbit went *lippitty-clippitty* through the woods to Brer Fox's house. When he got there he found Brer Terrapin sitting under a bush in the garden, just as he had told him to. And by him, on the ground, was a little string of bells! But Brer Terrapin wasn't ringing them yet.

Brer Rabbit hopped to the lighted window and looked in. He saw Brer Fox there, Brer Wolf and Brer Bear. On the table was a dish of raw carrots, raw turnips and onions, all waiting to be cooked in a stew. On the fire hung a big pan of boiling water. Was the chicken in there, cooking away? Brer Rabbit didn't think so, somehow!

He went to the door and knocked loudly – *blim-blam, blim-blam!* Brer Fox opened it and was full of delight to welcome Brer Rabbit.

"Well, you're nice and early!" he said. "The water's only just begun to boil – for the chicken, of course."

"Of course," agreed Brer Rabbit, sitting down.

Brer Fox sat down, too. "Well, what's the news?" said Brer Fox, throwing another log on the fire.

"Plenty of news tonight," said Brer Rabbit. "It's said that Brer Santa Claus is coming along this way with a mighty big sack of food for us all! What do you think of that?"

"There's a fine bit of news!" said Brer Bear. "I hope he'll have a pot or two of honey for me and my family."

"Sure to, Brer Bear, sure to!" said Brer Rabbit. "He's a kind and generous old fellow, Brer Santa Claus is! Oh, he'll be along soon, no doubt about it – he'll come in his sleigh with his galloping reindeer, and we'll hear his bells jingling out, so we shall!"

Just at that moment Brer Terrapin took up the string of bells he had beside him under the bush and shook them hard. The jingling came in at the window, and everyone sat up straight. *"Jingle-jingle-jingle! Jingle-jingle-jingle!"*

"There he is, for sure!" cried Brer Fox, and rushed to the door. Brer Terrapin went on ringing the bells like mad. Brer Bear and Brer Wolf ran to the door, too, and soon all three were out in the snow-covered garden.

"Sounds pretty near!" said Brer Fox, looking up into the sky, hoping to see Brer Santa Claus galloping along, ready to land on his roof. "Yes, pretty near!"

The bells certainly did sound pretty near, for they were just under the bush.

But Brer Fox didn't guess that! He and the others stood and waited for Brer Santa Claus to drop down from the sky.

Brer Terrapin crawled silently away from the bush, keeping well down under the snow. The bells sounded no more.

Brer Fox and the others felt cold and went indoors to get warm, and to see what Brer Rabbit was up to.

But Brer Rabbit wasn't there! Nor

were the carrots, the turnips or the onions! They had all disappeared with Brer Rabbit. But the pan of water was still boiling away merrily.

"Where's Brer Rabbit?" said Brer Bear. "And where's all the food?"

Brer Rabbit and the food were far away, waiting for old Brer Terrapin to come along out of the snow. And my, what a fine Christmas supper they both had, and what a fine laugh they had, too!

And when Brer Rabbit met Brer Fox the next day he shouted out to him. "Heyo, Brer Fox! Did Brer Santa Claus leave you a nice lot of presents? Sorry I couldn't wait to share them!"

Brer Fox rushed after him – but Brer Rabbit shot down a hole and laughed. Then he shook out a bit of string and jingled the bells on it.

"There's Brer Santa Claus again!" he shouted up the hole. "You go and join him, Brer Fox. That surely is Brer Santa Claus! *Jingle-jingle-jingle!*"

The clockwork kangaroo

The toys in Jackie's playroom were very happy together till the clockwork kangaroo came. Jackie had a big brown bear on wheels, a horse and a cart, a sailor doll, and a few other toys who lived together in the toy cupboard.

At night the sailor doll took the horse out of the cart, so that he could run free. In return the horse gave the doll a ride round the playroom. He loved to gallop about, and his hooves made a tiny pattering noise on the floor. Once when Jackie woke up, he heard the noise, but he thought it was the rain pattering outside! If he had looked into the playroom he would have seen that it was the horse.

The bear got the sailor doll to oil his wheels so that he could run quietly about at night without making any noise. The train didn't make much noise because it didn't run on its rails at night, but just anywhere it liked on the carpet.

And then the jumping kangaroo came. It was a very clever toy really, because its clockwork made it jump high in the air just as a real kangaroo does. How it could jump!

"Hallo!" said the kangaroo, the first night. "How are you all? I'm a jumping kangaroo."

"Oh, really, how interesting!" said the bear politely. "How far can you jump?"

"I'll show you," said the kangaroo. He sprang high into the air – and landed, bang, on the bear's nose!

"Please don't do that again," said the bear crossly, shaking the kangaroo off his nose.

The kangaroo sprang high into the air once more – and this time he landed on the engine of the train with such a crash that he bent the little funnel.

"Look what you've done!" said the train angrily. "I was very proud of my funnel. Now you've spoilt it. I don't look like a real train any more!"

The kangaroo leapt about till his clockwork was run down. Then, because no one would wind him up, he sat in a corner and sulked. He just couldn't reach his own key with his paws, which was a very good thing.

He made friends with Sam, a tiny doll whom nobody liked much, and Sam was always ready to wind him up. After that the toys didn't have a very good time at night, for the kangaroo was always jumping out at them from somewhere.

"He really is a *nuisance*," said the bear, rattling his four wheels crossly.

"So is Sam," said the sailor doll. "Always winding up the kangaroo so that he can jump on us."

"I wish the kangaroo had never come to our playroom," said the train. "We were as happy as could be before."

"Can't we get rid of him?" asked the horse. "Last night he jumped on my back and frightened me so much that I galloped three times round the playroom with him without stopping — and then he grinned and said, 'Thanks for the ride!' Horrid creature!"

"I wish he'd jump into the waste-paper basket!" said the bear. "That's deep — and he couldn't get out of there."

"Then he would be emptied into the dustbin the next morning and that would be the end of him," said the sailor doll. "That's an idea!"

"What do you mean?" asked the bear.

"I'll think of some plan with the waste-paper basket," said the doll. "Don't speak to me for a minute."

So he thought hard — and then he grinned round at the others. He looked round to make sure that the kangaroo was not near, and then he whispered to the others.

"Listen!" he said. "Tomorrow night we'll pretend to have a jumping-match to see who can jump the farthest. And when it comes to the kangaroo's turn to jump, we'll quickly swing out the basket – and he'll jump right into it."

"Oh, good!" said the bear. "Let's do it."

So the next night the toys all began talking about a jumping-match, and, of course, the kangaroo came along in great excitement, for he felt sure that he would be able to win the match easily.

"This is the jumping-off place," said the sailor doll, drawing a little line on the carpet with a piece of white chalk. "And we'll draw a white line to show where everyone jumps to – and the one who jumps the farthest shall win the prize."

"What is the prize?" asked the kangaroo at once.

"The prize is a chocolate," said the bear. The kangaroo was pleased. He wanted to have his turn first.

"No," said the bear. "Smallest ones first. Come on, Sam."

Sam stood on the chalk-line, grinning. He jumped – quite a good jump for such a tiny doll. The bear drew a chalk-line at the spot where he landed. "Now you, Ball!" he called. The red ball rolled up. It bounced off the chalk-line and did a very good jump indeed. The bear drew another line.

"That's fine, Ball," he said. "I believe you will win."

"No, he won't!" cried the kangaroo at once. "Let *me* try now!"

"It's not your turn," said the bear. "Train, come on."

The engine ran up and stood with its front wheels on the chalk-line. It gave a puff and jumped – but it fell right over on to its side with a clatter.

"Goodness! What a noise!" said the bear. "That wasn't a very good jump, Engine. Have you hurt yourself?"

"No," said the engine, and ran off into a corner on its six wheels to watch what was going to happen. The sailor doll jumped next – and his was a splendid jump, even better than the ball's. The kangaroo was so impatient to show that his jump would be even finer that he pushed everyone else out of the way and stood on the chalk-line himself, quite determined to win the prize.

"Now's the time to catch him!" whispered the bear to the sailor doll. "Where's the waste-paper basket?"

"I've got it ready under the table," whispered back the doll. "I'll go and push it out just as the kangaroo jumps! Don't say 'one, two, three, jump' till I'm ready."

The sailor doll ran under the table to the tall waste-paper basket. He took hold of it, ready to push it out. The bear saw that he was ready and counted for the kangaroo. "Are you ready? Now, one, two, three, JUMP!"

The kangaroo jumped. My, he did jump well! The doll saw him sailing through the air as if he had wings –

and then with a hard push the waste-paper basket was set right under the kangaroo – and he fell into it, plomp!

He was *most* surprised. He sat down on some apple-peel and torn-up paper and blinked his eyes in astonishment. "What's this?" he thought. "What's this?"

"Got him!" said the sailor doll in delight. All the toys danced round the basket in joy, except Sam, and he was cross. But he couldn't do anything at all.

"I say! I've fallen into the waste-paper basket," called the kangaroo, trying to scramble out. "This is most extraordinary."

"Yes, isn't it," giggled the sailor doll. "Didn't you see it there?"

"No, I didn't," said the kangaroo, puzzled. "It just seemed to come underneath me. I say, help me out, somebody."

But nobody did. Sam was too small to help, and the others wouldn't even try.

The kangaroo tried to jump out. He leapt higher and higher – but the basket was tall and he just couldn't jump over the top. He began to get frightened.

"My clockwork is nearly run down," he cried. "I can't jump out. Help me, do help me. I hate being mixed up with apple-peel, and paper, and dead flowers."

"Serves you right," said the bear gruffly. "You are a nuisance – and the right place for nuisances is the waste-paper basket or the dustbin."

The kangaroo began to cry. His clockwork had now run down and he could jump no more. He smelt of apple-peel. He was very unhappy because he knew that the basket was emptied into the dustbin every morning.

He began to scramble round and round the basket, like a goldfish swimming round a bowl. The toys giggled. The kangaroo had often frightened *them* – and now he was frightened himself. He would know what a horrid feeling it was.

Sam felt sorry for his friend, but he couldn't do anything to help him. "Oh, Kangy, I think the other toys have done this on purpose," he said sadly. "They have punished you for being naughty to them."

Well, the night went on, and the morning came – and Jane came to clean the playroom. She carried away the basket to empty it into the dustbin. And then the toys began to feel rather dreadful.

"I don't much like to think of Kangaroo in the smelly old dustbin," said the sailor doll. "What happens to things in the dustbin?"

"I don't know," said the bear. "Do you think he is very unhappy?"

Certainly the kangaroo was *most* unhappy. Jane had emptied him into the dustbin, and he had fallen on to a pile of wet tea-leaves, which stuck all over him.

"If only I had just one more jump left!" sighed the kangaroo sadly. "The next time anyone takes the lid off the dustbin I could jump out, for I am near the top."

Just as he spoke, Jane came to put some cinders there. She took off the lid and emptied the pan of cinders all over the kangaroo. He gathered himself together and did one last jump. Out he leapt – and Jane gave a yell.

"My gracious! What's this leaping about?"

She bent down and picked up the kangaroo. "Well, if it isn't the clockwork kangaroo. He must have got in here by mistake. I'll take him back to the playroom."

She took him back. Jackie wasn't there, so she put the dirty, cindery toy on the floor and left him there. He groaned, and the toys peeped out at him. At first they didn't know who it was, for the kangaroo was so dirty and so spotted with tea-leaves.

"Toys!" groaned the kangaroo. "Help me. I'm sorry I ever annoyed you. Do, do help me."

The toys were so pleased to think that the kangaroo was back that they all rushed to help him. They washed him. They brushed him. In fact, they couldn't do enough for him, and he almost cried for joy.

"It was dreadful in the dustbin," he said. "Really dreadful. Don't send me there any more. I'll never behave so badly again."

"Well, perhaps we've behaved badly too," said the sailor doll, ashamed. "You be kind to us, Kangaroo, and we'll be kind to you. There's nothing like kindness, you know."

Now the kangaroo never leaps on anyone, but instead he gives the sailor doll and Sam piggy-backs when he jumps – which is really *most* exciting for them. Didn't he have a horrid adventure?

The green plush duck

The green plush duck lived in the playroom with all the other toys. She had green plush wings, a green plush back, a red plush throat, a yellow beak and yellow legs; and a most beautiful voice that said "Quack!" very loudly when you pressed her in the middle.

Now none of the other toys had much voice. The teddy bear had only a very small growl because he had been so often pressed in the middle that his growl had nearly worn out. Emmeline, the baby doll, once had a voice that said "Mamma!" but when someone trod on her by accident one day her voice went wrong. And the rabbit never had a

growl or a squeak at all, though he pretended he had.

But, of course, when the playroom was in darkness and only the dying fire lighted up the room all the toys had lots to say! Their squeaks, growls and "Mammas" were only for the daytime — when day was gone they used their own proper little voices, and what a chatter there was!

Now it happened one evening that the green plush duck was feeling rather grand. Paul, the little boy the toys all belonged to, had had a friend to tea, and Margaret, the little friend, liked the plush duck best of all his toys. She had let the duck sit by her at teatime, and had made her quack quite a hundred times, if not more!

So no wonder the plush duck was feeling grand. Margaret had said that her quack was just like a real duck's and that she was the nicest duck in the world. So the plush duck was quite ready to be queen of the playroom that evening!

"Did you hear what Margaret said about me?" she said to the other toys. "She said my quack was . . ."

"Yes, we heard it," said the teddy bear, rather crossly. "We don't want to hear it again. Forget it, Duck."

"Forget it!" said the duck, in surprise. "Why should I forget it? I don't want to forget it, I want to remember it all my life. Why, Margaret said I was . . ."

"Oh do stop boasting!" said the rabbit. "And don't start quacking, for goodness sake. We've had enough of that awful noise today!"

"Well, I never! Awful noise indeed!" said the plush duck angrily. "Why, let me tell you this, Margaret said that I was the nicest duck in the world!"

"Well, you're not," said Emmeline, the doll. "Margaret can't have seen many ducks, or she wouldn't have said a silly thing like that. You're not a bit like a duck, not a bit! I have seen plenty of real live ducks, and they were all white.

You are a dreadful green colour, and you have a terrible quack that we're all tired of hearing, so now please be quiet."

Well, the plush duck was so angry to hear all that that she hardly knew what to say. Then she quacked very loudly indeed and said:

"So I'm not like a real duck, you say! Well, I am, so there! I can do everything a real duck can do, and I wish I *was* a real duck, so that I could live on the pond and not with nasty horrid toys like *you*!"

"Can you lay eggs?" asked the teddy bear.

"Of course not," said the plush duck.

"Well, a real duck can, so you're not like a real duck!" said the teddy.

"Can you swim?" asked the rabbit.

The plush duck didn't know. She had never tried.

"I expect so," she said at last. "I'm *sure* I could if I tried."

"Can you eat frogs?" asked Emmeline.

"Ooh, how horrid! I'm sure I don't want to!" said the plush duck, feeling quite ill.

"You can't lay eggs, you can't swim, you can't eat frogs, so you're not a *bit* like a real duck!" said the teddy. "Ha ha!"

"Ha ha!" said all the others.

The plush duck turned red with rage.

"I tell you I *am* like a real duck, only much nicer," she said. "I expect I *could* lay eggs and do everything else if I tried – but I've never tried."

"Well, try to lay an egg now," said Emmeline. So the plush duck solemnly sat down and tried hard to lay an egg. But it wasn't a bit of good, she couldn't. She was very disappointed.

"Well, eat a frog," said the rabbit.

"Get me one, and I will," said the plush duck. But nobody knew where to get a frog, or how to make it go to the playroom if they found one, so they told the plush duck they would take her word for that.

"Show us how you can swim," said the teddy.

"But where can I swim?" asked the duck. "There isn't a pond anywhere near, and the bathroom is too far away for us all to go there."

"You can swim in the tank belonging to the goldfish, up on that shelf there!" cried Emmeline, pointing to where the four goldfish swam slowly about in the big glass tank of water. But the plush duck didn't like the idea of that at all!

"Oh, I don't think I'll try tonight," she said. "The goldfish might not like it."

"You're afraid!" cried everyone. "You've told a story! You can't swim! You're not a *bit* like a real duck!"

This made the plush duck so angry that she at once climbed up to the shelf where the glass tank was, and popped into the water. For a moment or two she floated upright, and she was delighted.

"I *can* swim!" she called. But oh dear me, whatever was happening? Why, the water soaked into her plush skin and got right into the filling she was stuffed with. And she turned over and began to sink. How frightened she was – and how frightened the toys were too!

"Help, help!" cried the poor plush duck. "I'm sinking, I'm sinking! Help!"

The goldfish nibbled at her with their red mouths. The toys watched in horror. Whatever could they do? Then who do you think came forward to help? The three little plastic frogs that Paul floated in his bath each night! They had sat as quiet as could be all through the quarrel, because they were only small toys, and didn't like to speak. Also they had felt rather afraid in case the plush duck had offered to eat them instead of real frogs.

But they were brave, and they made up their minds to help. They jumped up to the shelf, and leapt into the tank of water. They dived underneath the poor frightened duck, and soon brought her to the surface again. The teddy and the rabbit pulled her out, and, dripping wet, she jumped down to the floor again.

"We're ever so sorry we teased you," said the bear, frightened. "Do forgive us."

"I'm not like a real duck," said the plush duck, sorrowfully. "I can't even swim."

"No, but you can quack," said the rabbit, anxious to make everything right again. "Quack, Duck, and let us hear your wonderful voice."

But what a dreadful thing! The water had got into the plush duck's quack, and she couldn't say a word. Not a single quack could she quack! She *was* upset. The water was very cold and she was shivering. The toys were afraid she would catch a dreadful cold, so they took her near the fire. The teddy was very brave and poked the fire well to make it flame up.

The duck gradually got dry, but she was still sad.

"I've not even got my quack now," she said with tears in her big glass eyes. "I can't swim, I can't lay eggs, I can't eat frogs, I can't even quack. I might as well be in the dustbin!"

"You mustn't say that!" said the toys, shocked. "Cheer up! We'll make you queen of the nursery, even if you *can't* quack!"

So they made the plush duck queen, but that didn't make her feel very happy, because she was so miserable about her lost quack.

But hip hurrah! In the morning when Paul came into the playroom to play, and pressed her in the middle, her quack had come back! "Quack!" she said, even more loudly than before! The water had dried out, and her quack was better than ever.

So now she is very happy. She is still queen of the playroom and her quack is just the same – but there's just one thing she won't do; she won't go anywhere near the tank of goldfish, and I'm not surprised, are you?

The elf in the playroom

Just outside the playroom window there was a climbing rose. It was very old, and had a thick twisted trunk, and hundreds and hundreds of leaves. In the summer it blossomed out, and was red with sweet-smelling roses.

In one of the thickest parts of the climbing rose lived a small elf called Lissome. She was a dear little thing with two long wings rather like a dragonfly's, which made a whirring noise when she flew.

Lissome was lonely, for no other elves lived in the garden. They were afraid of the two children who lived in the house. They were twin girls called Lucy and Jane, and they were rough and rude.

So no elves lived near them, except Lissome, who felt quite safe from them, high up in the climbing rose.

All the same it was a lonely life there. The sparrows sometimes came and talked to her. The robin had a song for her, and sometimes the summer butterflies and bees fluttered round and told her the news.

When she discovered that there were toys in the playroom who came alive at night and played merrily with each other, she was simply delighted!

She peeped in one night at the window and they all saw her!

"Look! An elf!" said the brown bear. "Let's ask her in!"

So in she flew on her long wings and smiled at all the wondering toys. There were the brown bear, the blue rabbit, three dolls, the black dog, the brown dog, and the pink cat. So there were a good many toys to play with!

Every night Lissome went to play in the playroom. All the toys loved her, for she was merry and kind. They played hide-and-seek, and catch, and hunt the slipper, and hunt the thimble, and a great many other games, too – the kind you play when you go to a party.

"You are lucky to be able to fly out of the window at dawn," said the brown bear one night. "We wish we could too!"

"Why?" said Lissome in surprise.

"Well, Lucy and Jane are such rough children," said the brown bear. "Look at my arm! It's almost off! The two children both wanted to play with me today, so they pulled and pulled – and my arm nearly came off! Whatever shall I do when it does?"

"I *am* sorry," said Lissome.

"And look at my tail," said the pink cat. "Lucy twisted it and twisted it today – and that's nearly off too. It may drop off at any minute! And who wants a cat without a tail?"

"You know, Toys, if you could lend me a needle and cotton, thimble and scissors, I think I could mend you," said Lissome. "I'm quite good at sewing."

"Are you really?" said the brown bear joyfully. "Well, here is the work-basket. It's got a lot of sewing things in it. Take what you want."

So Lissome took out a thimble which, however, was far too big, so she couldn't wear it. She took a tiny needle and threaded it, and she found a pair of scissors. Then she set to work.

She sewed the bear's arm beautifully. He was very pleased.

"It feels as firm as ever," he said, swinging it to and fro. Lissome took the scissors and snipped the cotton.

"Now I'll do the pink cat's tail," she said. The pink cat at once turned round backwards, and Lissome threaded the needle with pink silk to sew on the tail.

Now the blue rabbit had been watching everything with great interest. He couldn't sew — but he did wish he might use those scissors!

Snip, snip, they went, and he wished he could make them go snip, snip, too!

"Let me snip the cotton next time," he begged. So Lissome said he might. He picked up the scissors and put them ready. He snip-snipped them in the air just to practise using them – and then a dreadful thing happened!

He snip-snipped the scissors too near Lissome the elf – and she stepped back just at that moment – and the blue rabbit snipped off one of her lovely wings!

"Oooooh!" cried Lissome in fright. She turned round and saw her lovely wing on the floor. The blue rabbit burst into sobs. He was terribly upset and unhappy.

"Forgive me, forgive me!" he wept. "I didn't mean to. Oh, what shall I do, what shall I do?"

"You wicked, careless rabbit!" cried the pink cat, who saw how pale the elf had gone. "Just when Lissome is doing a kind turn to us you go and snip off one of her beautiful wings!"

"I didn't mean to, I tell you – I didn't mean to!" howled the rabbit, more upset than he had ever been in his life before.

Lissome patted him gently. "Don't cry so," she said. "It was an accident."

"But what will you do?" wept the blue rabbit. "You can't fly now."

"Well, I must just stay in my rose-home until my wing has grown again," said the elf.

"Oh, will it grow again?" cried everyone joyfully. Nobody had thought of that.

"Of course," said the elf. "It will only take a week. So cheer up, Rabbit."

He did cheer up. He squeezed out his wet hanky and tried to smile. Then something else came into his mind, and he looked miserable again.

"*Now* what's the matter?" said the elf.

"I've just thought – you can't fly out of the window tonight," said the rabbit. "So what will you do?"

"Oh, dear," said the elf. "I hadn't thought of that. Can I climb up somehow?"

"No. There's nothing to climb on," said the pink cat. "There's no chair by the window, and we are not big enough to put one there. Rabbit – use your brains. You got Lissome into this muddle. Now get her out of it! Go on – use your brains, if you've got any, or we'll all be very angry with you."

The rabbit thought hard. "We'll hide her!" he said.

"Don't be silly," said the brown bear. "You know that the playroom is turned out tomorrow. There won't be a single corner that isn't swept."

"Put her in the brick-box," said the brown dog.

"Yes – and let Lucy and Jane find her if they use their bricks tomorrow!" said the pink cat scornfully. "And if they treat *us* roughly, what do you suppose they will do to a little elf like Lissome? They would make her *very* unhappy!"

"The brick-box has given me an idea!" said the blue rabbit suddenly. "Let's get all the bricks out — and build a high castle up to the window-sill! Then Lissome can walk up the bricks and climb out to her home!"

"Now that really *is* a good idea!" said the brown bear, and he went to the big brick box. He and the rabbit emptied out the bricks on the floor, and then all the toys began to build a high castle to the window-sill.

It took ages, because the toys were not very good at building, and the bricks kept tumbling down. But at last the castle was done, and just reached the sill!

"It's dawn now!" whispered Lissome, and she climbed up the bricks. "You must sleep, or you will be seen running around. Thank you for your help, Toys! I'll come again when my wing has grown."

The toys heard someone moving about downstairs. Someone was up!

They scuttled into the toy cupboard and shut the door. "We've left the bricks out!" whispered the rabbit, and he lay quite still in a corner. "Oh, dear!"

Well, there wasn't time to put them back into the box, for Lucy and Jane were now both awake and dressing. They rushed into the playroom – and *how* astonished they were to see the bricks leading up to the window-sill!

"Who's built that?" said Lucy.

"And what for?" said Jane.

"The *toys* can't have done it!" said Lucy. "How I'd like to know what it's there for!"

But she never did know. As for the elf, her wing grew again in seven days, and she fluttered in at the window once more, as merry as ever. But she wouldn't let the blue rabbit use the scissors again – and I'm not surprised, are you?

179

Buttercup magic

N ow, one morning, old Mother Doodah went across the buttercup field with her shopping. She had a very full basket, and on the top of it was a pat of lovely golden butter that she had bought from the butter-woman in the market.

Mother Doodah put her basket down to do up her shoe. She didn't see that the pound of butter had slipped down into the buttercups. She got up again, and went off with her shopping – but the butter lay in the field, as golden as the buttercups.

Who should come along but the four naughty little imps who lived at the bottom of the field in an old hollow

tree. One of them tripped over the butter.

"What's this?" said Higgle.

"Butter!" said Piggle, poking it.

"What a lot!" said Tick, and he tried to pick it up, but it was almost as big as he was.

"We'll take it home," said Tock. "I wonder who dropped it?"

"Mother Doodah, I expect," said Higgle. "She always brings her shopping back across this field."

Not one of them thought of running after Mother Doodah to ask her if she had dropped the butter. Higgle poked his finger right through the paper and into the butter. "Oooh – isn't it lovely!"

He had butter on his finger and he licked it off.

"Don't do that," said Piggle. "It's not your butter!"

" 'Tis!" said Higgle. "I found it. Don't talk to me like that, Piggle, or I shan't let you have even a lick." He poked his finger into the butter, and licked it again.

Tick poked his finger in, too, but Higgle pushed him away. "You can only do that if I say so," he said. "It's *my* butter. I found it."

"You didn't! You only tripped over it!" said Tick. "Mean thing!"

"You're always mean," said Tock, and he gave Higgle a push that sent him almost headfirst into the butter.

"Now then, stop that!" said Higgle, looking very fierce. "I tell you, this is *my butter*, and if any of you behave badly to me you won't get any of it. Not a lick!"

Piggle, Tick and Tock shouted angrily at him, but they didn't dare to touch the butter again. Higgle could be very fierce when he wanted to.

And then a voice came from behind them. "Now, now – what's all this quarrelling? What is the noise about? I was having a nap and you disturbed me!"

The four imps turned round and saw Sly the goblin. Higgle pointed to the butter.

"See that butter? I found it. So it's mine, isn't it? You say it's mine, Sly, and I'll give you a big piece."

"Now, now," said Sly. "We can easily find out whose this butter is. Very easily indeed. I'm quite sure that you don't *all* like butter, do you? Quite a lot of imps never even eat it."

"I like it!" cried Higgle, and the others said the same.

"Well, we'll prove it," said Sly. "I don't expect more than one of you likes butter, and if Higgle found the butter I daresay he's the one that likes it. If I find any one of you others liking it, well, you shall have a share, too."

"But how are you going to find out who likes butter and who doesn't?" said Higgle, impatiently. "I think this is silly. The butter's mine."

" 'Tisn't!" yelled the others. "We *all*

found it. You just happened to trip over it!"

"Be quiet," said Sly, sternly. "I will now show you the old, old way of finding out who likes butter. It was discovered by my great-great-great-grandma about four hundred years ago!"

The imps looked at him in surprise. "Show us," they said.

Sly picked a golden buttercup. "Watch," he said, and he tilted up his chin, and looked up into the sky. "I'm going to hold this buttercup under my chin. If a gold patch comes under my chin, as yellow as butter, that shows I like butter. Will you please look and see if I do?"

The imps crowded near to look. They saw a bright gold patch spreading under the goblin's chin, reflected from the buttercup.

"You like butter, yes, you do. Very, very much!" called the imps. "Now do that to us! See if *we* like butter, too.

And if we all do, we *all* share the butter, don't we?"

"Yes, yes. Don't make such a noise," said Sly. "Now, please do what I say. Sit down in a ring, with your backs to each other. Tilt up your chins, and look straight up at the sky. And sit like that and wait till I come round with the buttercup. I'll hold it under your chins and at the end I'll tell you what I see."

So the four imps did as they were told and sat in a ring, their backs to one another. They tilted up their chins and looked right up into the sky.

They waited, and they waited. Their necks began to feel stiff, but still they waited. What a long time Sly was taking over finding out who liked butter!

At last Higgle couldn't hold up his head any longer. He put his chin down and looked round for Sly. But Sly wasn't there!

"The *butter's* not there, either!" shouted Higgle, and that made the other three imps put their chins down, too, and look round in astonishment.

"Sly's gone – and so has the butter!" cried Higgle. "Oh, the wretch! Oh, the rogue! He didn't mean to find out if we liked butter at all! He just meant to go off with it himself. Why did we quarrel about it? Why didn't we remember that Sly loves butter with his bread?"

"After him! After him!" shouted Tick, and all four imps raced across the field, under the stile and into the next field, where they knew Sly lived.

But they hadn't gone very far into the next field when they heard an angry voice. It was Mother Doodah's. The imps peeped through the long grasses and the tall buttercups.

Mother Doodah was holding Sly by the collar and she was shaking him so hard that the imps could hear his teeth rattling in his head. Shake, shake, shake! Rattle, rattle!

"What do you mean, running off with my butter? *I* saw you, slinking through the grasses with it, you wicked little goblin!" Shake, shake, shake!

"I didn't take it, it was the four imps, *they* found it!" wept Sly. "I was taking it back to you, really I was!"

"Oh, you were, were you – and dipping your finger into it all the way and sucking off the butter!" cried the angry old woman. "Well, if I catch those four imps I'll ask them if what you say is true – and if it is, they'll get a shaking as well as you!" Shake, shake, shake! Rattle, rattle!

The four imps ran off as fast as ever they could. Dear, dear – to think that Sly had been caught by Mother Doodah like that!

"It serves him right," said Higgle, when they were safely in their hollow tree.

"Well – it might have happened to *us*," said Piggle. "I think now we should have run after Mother Doodah and given the butter back to her."

"We certainly should," said Tick, remembering how Mother Doodah had shaken Sly.

"We will another time," said Tock. "Ha, ha! I *shall* laugh at Sly next time I see him."

Poor Sly had been shaken almost to bits, and he had gone to Old Man Jigsaw to be put together properly again, so they didn't see him for a very long time.

The funny thing is, of course, that he was quite right about buttercups showing who likes butter! The little bit of magic in them still works. Hold one under your friend's chin, and see whether the little golden patch shows there, or not.

It's really rather strange, isn't it?

The talking shoes

Once there was a little girl called Jennifer. She walked a mile to school each day and back, and that was quite a long way. Sometimes it rained and then she took her mac. Sometimes it was cold and she took her coat – and sometimes it was very hot and she wore no coat at all, but a shady hat in case she got sunstroke.

One day she set out in the sunshine. It was a nice, sunny, autumn day. Jennifer had a short coat on, and her lace-up shoes, and her school hat. She ran along, singing a song she was learning at school.

Half-way to school a great black cloud came up and it began to pour

with rain. How it poured! You should
have seen it. The rain came down
like slanting lines of silver, and big
puddles came all along the road.

Jennifer stood under a tree to shelter
herself. When the rain stopped she ran
out into the road again – and stepped
right into a most enormous puddle! It
was deeper than her ankles – so she
wetted her shoes and socks dreadfully.

"Good gracious!" said Jennifer, in

dismay. "Now look what I've done! I shall have to sit in school with wet shoes and socks all morning, and I shall get an awful cold."

She walked along very sadly, thinking of how she would sneeze and cough the next day – and then she passed by a little yellow cottage where a dear old lady lived all alone. The old lady was shaking the crumbs off her tablecloth for the birds in the garden, and she called to Jennifer, who knew her well.

"Did you get caught in that rainstorm, my dear?"

"Yes, I did," said Jennifer sadly. "And just look at my shoes and socks! I stepped into a puddle, and they are wet through!"

"Dear me, that's very dangerous," said the old woman at once. "Come along in and I'll see if I can lend you a pair of my stockings, and a dry pair of shoes. I have a very small foot, so maybe I can manage something for you."

So Jennifer went into the tidy little cottage, and the old lady found a pair of lace-up shoes for Jennifer, and a pair of stockings.

"There!" she said. "These will do nicely. I can lend you a pair of garters, too, to keep up the stockings. Put them on, my dear, and I will dry your wet things and have them ready for you by the time you pass by at dinner-time."

Jennifer put on the stockings. Then she put on the shoes. They had big tongues to them, and long laces, but they were most comfortable. They felt nice and dry too.

"Thank you," said Jennifer gratefully. "I'll try not to tread in any more puddles with these on."

She skipped off to school. The old lady stood at the gate and called after her. "Oh – Jennifer dear – just a minute. Don't be naughty at school today, will you? You may be sorry if you are!"

"How funny!" thought Jennifer. "Why should I have to be specially good today? *I* don't know."

Jennifer was not very good at school. She whispered and talked when she shouldn't. She made a mess in her writing book instead of keeping it nice and tidy. She pulled the plaits of the little girl in front, and she pinched the boy next to her because she didn't like him. So you see she really wasn't a very good child at school.

She didn't see any real reason why she should be good that day. So she didn't try. She picked up her number book so roughly that a page tore in half.

Then a funny thing happened. A voice spoke in the silence of the classroom — a rather deepdown, husky voice that no one had ever heard before.

"Careless girl, isn't she?" said the voice. "Did you see how she tore her number book?"

"Yes, I did," said another voice, just as deepdown and husky. "She ought to lose a mark for that."

"Who is talking?" asked Miss Brown in astonishment, looking round the class. The voices didn't sound a bit like any of the girls' voices. The children stared round in amazement. Jennifer went red. How dare somebody talk about her like that?

She wondered if it was the little boy next to her. She pinched him slyly. A voice spoke loudly again.

"Did you see Jennifer pinch the little boy next to her? Isn't she cruel?"

"A most unkind child," said the second voice. "I don't think I like her."

"Oh! Who's talking like that about me!" cried Jennifer in a rage.

"It sounds like somebody on the ground," said Miss Brown, puzzled and alarmed. Everyone looked on the floor. Nobody was hiding beneath the tables or desks.

Have you guessed what it was that was talking? Perhaps you have! It was the tongues in the two borrowed shoes! They chattered away to one another, and were most surprising to hear.

"I think she has a very cross face, don't you?" said one tongue. "It's a pity she doesn't look in the mirror. Then she would see how horrid she looks when she keeps frowning."

"Will you stop talking, whoever it is?" cried Miss Brown, and she rapped on her desk.

The shoes held their tongues and stopped talking for a while. They were frightened of Miss Brown. The class settled down to write. They were copying from the blackboard. Jennifer did not try very hard. When she opened her desk to get out her pen her book slid to the floor.

"Good gracious!" said one tongue to the other. "Just look at Jennifer's dreadful writing! Did you ever see anything so awful for a child of ten?

Really, she ought to be ashamed of herself."

"Poor thing! Perhaps she can't write any better," said the other tongue, flapping itself a little. "Look at that mistake! If I were the teacher, I would put Jennifer into the corner."

"Oh! Oh!" cried Jennifer, stamping her foot and bursting into tears. "I won't stand it! Who is saying these horrid things about me?"

"I can't imagine, Jenny," said Miss Brown. "All I can say is that the things are perfectly true! It is a shocking thing that a girl of ten should write so badly and be so untidy."

Jennifer picked up her book sulkily and put it on her desk. The shoes chatted together again.

"She's got her horrid, sulky face on now. Isn't she a most unpleasant child? I wonder how many mistakes she will make on her next page!"

Jennifer set her teeth and made up her mind to make no mistakes at all. She wrote a really beautiful page and showed it to Miss Brown.

"Good gracious, Jennifer! I've never seen such nice writing from you before!" cried Miss Brown.

"You see, she *can* do it if she tries," said one shoe. "She's just too lazy to do it always."

"I'm not lazy, I'm not lazy!" cried Jennifer, and she stamped her foot. That gave the shoes such a shock that they said nothing at all for a whole hour. Then it was geography, a lesson that Jennifer didn't like. She leaned over and pulled the plaits of the little girl in front of her. The little girl squealed.

"Somebody pulled my hair!" she cried. Miss Brown looked up crossly.

"Was it you, Jenny?" she asked.

"No, Miss Brown," said Jennifer untruthfully.

"OoooooooooOOOOOH!" said one shoe to the other. "Isn't she untruthful? Really! Ooooooooh!"

"Untruthful, cowardly and unkind," said the other shoe. "Why doesn't somebody send her to bed?"

Jennifer glared round at everyone, thinking that *somebody* must be playing a trick on her, talking like this. But everyone was as astonished as she was.

"Who *is* talking?" cried Miss Brown, quite alarmed again. "I don't like this. I shall put the talkers into the corner if I hear any more."

"Fancy! She'd put us in the corner!" giggled a shoe. "Well, she'd have to put Jenny there, too, if she put us."

"Perhaps we'd better not talk," said the other shoe. "I believe we are disturbing the class a little. Sh!"

So they said no more until it was time to go home. Then Jennifer went sulkily to the cloakroom and took down her hat and coat. Another child got in her way, and she gave him a push that knocked him right over.

"Isn't she rough?" said the shoe,

shocked. "Did you see her push that nice little boy right over? If she did that to me, I'd kick her!"

"And I'd trip her up!" said the other shoe fiercely. "Horrid girl! Do you suppose anyone in the world likes her at all?"

"I expect her mother does," said the first shoe. "Mothers are funny – they always love their children even when the children are horrid and rude to them. I should think Jennifer is rude to her mother, wouldn't you?"

Jenny sat down on a bench and began to cry. "I'm *not* rude to my mother, I'm not, I'm not," she wept. "I love her. I'm kind to her. Oh, who is it saying these unkind things about me? I may behave horribly sometimes, but I *can* be good when I try!"

"I don't believe that, do you?" said one shoe.

"No," said the other. "She couldn't be good! She's one of these spoilt children we've heard about."

The other children laughed. They were sorry for Jennifer, but they couldn't help thinking that it would do her good to hear these things. She went off crying bitterly, puzzled and unhappy.

The shoes talked on and on. They chatted about Jenny's bad writing and her wrong sums and her pinching and pushing. Jenny sobbed and cried all the way to the little yellow cottage. The old lady was waiting for her at the gate.

"Dear, dear!" she said, when she saw Jenny coming along with red eyes and tear-stained cheeks. "What's the matter? Have those shoes been wagging their tongues too much?"

"Shoes? Wagging their tongues?" said Jenny in amazement. "What do you mean?"

"Well, those shoes I lent you this morning can be most tiresome," said the old lady. "They belonged to my great-grandmother, you know, and were made by a brownie, so it is said. They have tongues, of course, just as your own lace-up shoes have – but these shoe tongues can talk – and talk they do! They are real chatterboxes. I hope they didn't say anything unkind!"

"Oh, no, we only spoke the truth!" cried the two shoe tongues together, and they flapped themselves about in the shoes. Jenny looked down in amazement. She took off the shoes very quickly indeed.

"So they were the talkers!" she said. "The tongues of my shoes! Well – I never knew shoe tongues could talk!"

"Oh, my dear, they all could at one time," said the old lady. "That is why they were called tongues, you know, because they spoke. But they did say the silliest, most tiresome things, so now very few of them are allowed to talk. I can't stop the tongues in this pair of shoes, though.

That's why I called to you to be good this morning – because I knew the shoe tongues would talk about it if you were naughty."

"I shan't be *quite* so naughty in future," said Jenny, beginning to smile. "I don't like to be thought lazy and stupid and horrid. Lend me your shoes in a month's time, and see if they can say heaps of *nice* things about me for a change, will you?"

"Certainly," said the old lady, slipping Jenny's own shoes on her feet. "How cross they will be if there is nothing naughty they can chat about!"

I'd like to hear what they say in a month's time, wouldn't you? What would *your* shoe tongues say if they could speak, I wonder? Do tell me!

Brer Rabbit's Easter eggs

O ne day, not very far off Easter, Brer Rabbit sauntered round his garden to see how his seeds were getting on. The birds were pecking at some of them so he thought he'd put up a scarecrow.

"I'll get some hay and stuff an old sack," said Brer Rabbit to himself. And off he went to the haystack.

He had only just put his hand in to pull out some hay, when he felt something hard. "Now, what's this?" he said. "Feels like eggs to me."

He made a hole to see what it was, and, sure enough, there was a cosy little nest of chicken eggs. But goodness knows how long they had been there, and Brer Rabbit knew they would be as stale as stale.

"No use," he said, sorrowfully. "No use at all. They'll be as bad as can be."

He took them out and counted them. There were six, all fine big ones, and Brer Rabbit reckoned it was a great pity that he hadn't found them before.

Then a thought came to him. He couldn't eat them himself, for he was certain they were bad – but no one else knew that, and he could give them to Brer Fox or Brer Bear, and

tell them to make an Easter pudding of them! Then, oh my! Wouldn't they pull a face when they found what the pudding tasted like!

He went indoors with them, and put them into a basket. Then he covered them neatly with a cloth, and set out to go to Brer Bear's, for he guessed Brer Fox wouldn't believe him if he said they were fresh eggs.

Brer Bear was standing at his door when Brer Rabbit arrived.

"Good day," he said. "What have you got in that basket?"

"Eggs," said Brer Rabbit. "Beautiful new-laid eggs. Brown and big – oh, fit for a king, these eggs are."

"Who are they for?" asked Brer Bear.

"They're for *you*!" said Brer Rabbit, beaming all over his face. "They're my Easter present to you. I hope you'll accept them Brer Bear, with my best wishes."

Brer Bear was so surprised he couldn't think what to say. It wasn't like

Brer Rabbit to go about giving presents, and Brer Bear wondered if there was any trick in it.

"Do you want me to give you anything for them?" he asked at last.

"*Give* me anything!" said Brer Rabbit, in a hurt sort of voice. "Of course not! Haven't I just told you these are my Easter present to you, Brer Bear? You take them and make an Easter pudding for yourself. I'm fond of you, so I've brought you my best eggs."

"Thank you, Brer Rabbit," said Brer Bear. "It's very kind of you, I'm sure."

He took the basket, and put the eggs on a dish. Then he gave the basket back to Brer Rabbit, and thanked him again.

"Don't say another word about it!" said Brer Rabbit, graciously. "I wish you a happy Easter!"

With that he ran off through the wood, chuckling to himself whenever he thought of Brer Bear using those eggs.

Now Brer Bear kept hens himself, and that evening when he went to see if there were any eggs, he found many more than usual. He brought them indoors, and put them on a dish beside those that Brer Rabbit had brought him.

"Too many eggs!" he said, looking at them. "I shall never eat them all. I'd better give some away! If Brer Rabbit's going about giving Easter presents, then I'd better, too."

So the next morning he put on his coat, and went to call on Brer Wolf.

Brer Wolf was in the garden, and Brer Bear sang out to him:

"Heyo, Brer Wolf! Here's a present for you."

Brer Wolf looked at Brer Bear, and wondered what he was up to. But Brer Bear looked so amiable and talked so kindly that soon Brer Wolf forgot to wonder about him, and took the eggs.

"They're just an Easter present," said Brer Bear. "You make an Easter pudding for yourself, Brer Wolf, and enjoy it. I've so many eggs that I'm glad to be able to give you these."

"Thank you kindly, Brer Bear," said Brer Wolf. He took the eggs out of the basket and put them in a bowl. Then he gave Brer Bear's bag back to him, and saw him out of the garden, thinking that old Brer Bear was certainly a good fellow, even if he *had* done some mighty queer things in his time.

Now that night Brer Wolf was taken ill, and when the doctor came he said that Brer Wolf had been eating too much.

"You just eat nothing but bread and water for a week," said the doctor, "or you'll certainly die. You've been greedy, Brer Wolf, that's what you've been, and you're all upset inside, worse than anyone I've ever seen."

"Oh, my!" said Brer Wolf, frightened almost out of his wits. "I promise you I'll be careful, doctor. But what am I to do with those lovely eggs over there? I've only just been given them, and surely *they* won't hurt me if I eat them?"

"They'll kill you, sure enough, Brer Wolf," said the doctor. "You give those eggs away, and don't get tempted by them, or you'll be dead this time tomorrow."

Well, Brer Wolf had only bread and water for two days, and then he got so hungry that the sight of those eggs gave him a pain.

"If I don't give them away quick as quick, I'll eat them, that's sure," he said. So he put on his hat, and took the eggs with him in a basket.

"I'll give them to Brer Fox," he decided. "He's been a good friend to me, and maybe he'll be sorry for me and give me something back for them."

Brer Fox was having a snooze on his bed, when Brer Wolf knocked on his door. He jumped up in a mighty hurry, and shouted to know who it was.

"It's Brer Wolf," said Brer Wolf. "I've brought you a present of some eggs, Brer Fox."

Brer Fox wasn't pleased to hear this, for he didn't like eggs. But he was never one to say no to a present, so Brer Wolf gave him the eggs, and told him to make himself a nice Easter pudding with them.

"Thank you, Brer Wolf," said Brer Fox, putting them into his pocket. "I hope you'll soon be able to eat a good meal."

"Oh, so do I," said Brer Wolf, and he was just going to sit down and tell Brer Fox all his troubles, when Brer Fox opened the door for him to go.

"I've got to go and see someone," said Brer Fox, who didn't want to listen to any troubles of Brer Wolf's. "You get home quickly, Brer Wolf. You look very poorly, you do – as if you were going to die, or something."

That frightened Brer Wolf, and he hurried home as fast as he could, and put himself to bed with dreadful groans.

Brer Fox took the eggs from his pocket and looked at them.

"What shall I do with them?" he wondered. "Shall I take them to Brer Rabbit's, and sell them to him cheap? I know he's fond of them."

Then a fine idea came to him. He got some red and green ink, and painted the eggs very bright colours.

"It's Easter tomorrow, and Brer Rabbit'll be wanting Easter eggs for his old woman and her children," he chuckled. "He'll buy these all right, and I'll put some money in my pocket!"

When they were dry, he went off to Brer Rabbit's. He knocked at the door, and Brer Rabbit popped his head out of the window.

"Heyo, Brer Rabbit," said Brer Fox. "Do you want any Easter eggs for your old woman? Look! I've got some fine ones!"

He took them out of his pocket, and held them up for Brer Rabbit to see.

"I don't think much of them," said Brer Rabbit. "How much are they?"

"Five pence each," said Brer Fox. "Very cheap too."

"Oh no they're not," said Brer Rabbit. "You give me them for a two pence each, and I'll buy them."

"Certainly not," said Brer Fox, and he pretended he was going off in a temper.

Well they higgled and haggled first one way and then another, and at last Brer Rabbit took the eggs, and gave Brer Fox a two pence each for them.

But Brer Fox got a fine cabbage out of Brer Rabbit as well, and he picked it himself, for Brer Rabbit wasn't going to come out and pick it, not he! He thought Brer Fox had a nasty hungry look about him.

Well, the next morning Brer Rabbit gave the eggs to his old woman, and told her to make a fine Easter pudding out of them.

When she broke them, they smelt dreadful, but she reckoned it was only the paint they were daubed with. So she served the pudding up to Brer Rabbit for his dinner, and said nothing.

Brer Rabbit took a huge spoonful and swallowed it – and then, oh, my! He sat and choked and choked and spluttered and spluttered as if he was going to die that very minute.

"These eggs are bad, as bad as any eggs could be," he shouted to his old woman. "And I'm a-going to tell Brer Fox what I think of him!"

He ran straight out, and went to Brer Fox's, coughing and choking all the way. Brer Fox was surprised to see him, and told him that Brer Wolf had given him the eggs, so he'd better go and grumble at *him*, if he wanted to make himself unpleasant.

Brer Fox had such a nasty gleam in his eye that Brer Rabbit reckoned he'd better go on to Brer Wolf's after all. But Brer Wolf, who was in bed, told him that Brer Bear had given him the eggs.

"You go along to old Brer Bear and tell him he's no friend of mine!" said Brer Wolf, when he heard how bad the eggs were. "Why, he might have poisoned me!"

So Brer Rabbit ran panting to Brer Bear's, meaning to give him such a dressing-down as he'd never had in his life before.

Brer Bear was just going to go out walking when Brer Rabbit arrived, and mighty surprised he was to find himself pummelled and punched by Brer Rabbit, in a perfect fury.

"I'll teach you to send bad eggs about!" cried Brer Rabbit. "And Brer Wolf says you might have poisoned him, so you're no friend to him, he

says! They came round to me, and my stars and moon, they were so bad they nearly killed me!"

Then all of a sudden Brer Bear sat down and began to laugh. He laughed and laughed, till Brer Rabbit had to stop punching him, and ask him what was the matter.

"Oh, you'll be the death of me, you will, Brer Rabbit!" said Brer Bear, wiping his eyes. "Why, those eggs that I gave Brer Wolf, and which came round to you, were the very ones you so kindly brought me for an Easter present! Oh, Brer Rabbit, you've been punished this time all right! If you want to kick anybody, you just go and kick yourself!"

Well, Brer Rabbit didn't wait to hear any more. He ran straight back home, and poured the pudding down the sink. Then he went to bed and thought very hard. And soon Brer Bear, Brer Wolf, and Brer Fox came under his window and laughed *very* loud indeed.

Brer Rabbit's honey

Now one day, when Brer Rabbit went to get a pot of honey out of his shed, he saw that half of it was gone.

"Look at that, now!" said Brer Rabbit, very angry. "Who's been stealing my honey pots? Yes – one, two, three, four, five, six of them. All gone. Only three left!"

Brer Rabbit stood still a minute, and then he looked in the mud outside the door. In the mud he saw the print of Brer Bear's big feet, claws and all.

"Oho, Brer Bear, so *you've* been along here after my honey, have you?" said Brer Rabbit, to himself. "Well, you think yourself mighty clever, don't you, taking honey from old Brer Rabbit. But

I'll get it back, or I'll eat my whiskers!"

So Brer Rabbit hid himself outside Brer Bear's house, waiting for old Brer Bear to go walking out, so that he might slip inside and find his pots of honey. But whenever Brer Bear stepped out, he left old Mrs Bear behind in the house – and she was every bit as big and fierce as Brer Bear himself.

"This won't do," said Brer Rabbit to himself. "If I don't get that honey soon, it'll be gone – and I'll have to eat my own whiskers."

He sat and thought. He scratched his head, and pulled at his whiskers. Then he slapped his knee, and gave a grin. It didn't take Brer Rabbit long to think of a trick – he was just full of them, any time of night or day!

Old Brer Rabbit ambled off till he came to the riverside. He whistled, and up came Uncle Mud-Turtle, a-bubbling under the water.

"Good morning to you," said Brer Rabbit. "I'd take it mighty kind of you if you'd do something for me, Uncle Mud-Turtle."

"I'll bubble-bubble-bubble do it," answered Uncle Mud-Turtle.

"Well, listen, now," said Brer Rabbit. "There's a mighty cosy hole just here, and I want you to sit in it, Uncle Mud-Turtle, and if anything comes down this hole, well, you just hold on to it for all your worth. See? You just do that, and I'll give you a taste of the finest honey you ever sipped!"

"Bubble-bubble," answered Uncle Mud-Turtle. He got himself into the cosy hole by the bank and settled down comfortably to wait. Brer Rabbit sat by the hole too, and he watched till he saw Brer Bear coming out of his house. Then Brer Rabbit began to whistle very gently, as if he was humming a tune all to himself.

Brer Bear heard him and came through the bushes. He saw Brer Rabbit with his paw just coming out of the hole, and spoke to him.

"What are you doing there, Brer Rabbit?"

"Oh, is it you, Brer Bear?" said Brer Rabbit, standing up quickly and brushing himself down. "I wasn't doing anything much."

"You just tell me what you were doing now, Brer Rabbit," said Brer Bear, moving closer.

"Well, don't you tell anyone if I tell you, Brer Bear," begged Brer Rabbit.

"You go on and tell me," said Brer Bear.

"Well, Brer Bear, it's like this," said cunning old Brer Rabbit. "Someone has been stealing my honey. It might be Brer Fox and it might be Brer Wolf. So I'm looking for a place to hide it safely. Would you think this hole a good place, Brer Bear?"

"Oh, a mighty good place," said Brer Bear at once. "Have you put any there yet, Brer Rabbit?"

"Oh, I shan't tell you *that*," said Brer Rabbit. "You won't go and tell anyone, will you, Brer Bear?"

"Not I," said Brer Bear, making up his mind to look in that hole as soon as Brer Rabbit had gone.

"Well, goodbye, Brer Bear. So nice to have seen you. *Such* a surprise!" said Brer Rabbit, and he skipped nimbly away into the bushes. He hid behind a tree and watched.

Brer Bear waited for a minute or two and then he went to the hole. He sniffed around it, and then put his big paw down to feel about for pots of honey.

And Uncle Mud-Turtle got hold of it and bit it hard! My, how he bit it! And he held on for all he was worth, biting away like a trap!

Brer Bear began to howl. He tried to get his paw out, but Uncle Mud-Turtle bit harder. Brer Bear lifted his head and yowled like fifty dogs and cats at once. Brer Rabbit slipped to Brer Bear's house and knocked on the door. Mrs Bear opened it.

"Mrs Bear, quick! Brer Bear's shouting for you!" cried Brer Rabbit.

"But he said I wasn't to leave the house," said Mrs Bear.

"Well, you listen to him," said Brer Rabbit.

So Mrs Bear listened, and when she heard the shouts and yells, the screeches and the howls, she set off down the path to the river just as fast as she could go, crying, "I'm a-coming, I'm a-coming!"

And then Brer Rabbit popped in at Brer Bear's door, saw his honey-pots on the shelf, put them into a basket, and ran out with them. On his way by the river he spied Brer Bear and Mrs Bear coming towards him. Brer Bear was nursing his right paw, and howling and crying.

"Why, Brer Bear, what's wrong?" cried Brer Rabbit, standing at a safe distance.

"What's wrong? Plenty wrong!" shouted back Brer Bear. "There's a wild animal down that hole, that's what's wrong. He's eaten your honey, sure enough!"

"Well, I've plenty here!" yelled back Brer Rabbit, and he held up his basket of pots.

Brer Bear knew the basket – and he knew the pots! He gave a yell and rushed towards Brer Rabbit. "You give me back that honey!" he shouted.

"I'll hide it down that hole!" cried Brer Rabbit, dodging away. "You go look for it there, Brer Bear!"

And the funny thing was that old Brer Rabbit *did* hide his honey down that hole – for he guessed that Brer Bear would never dare to put his paw down there again, so it would be as safe there as anywhere!

As for Uncle Mud-Turtle, he got his spoonful of honey, but he laughed so much when he took it that he choked and Brer Rabbit had to bang him on the back, and nearly broke his shell! Well, well – you never know what old Brer Rabbit will be up to next!

The dog with the very long tail

There was once a dog with a very long tail. His name was Ginger, because he was just the colour of ginger, and he belonged to little Terry Brown.

Terry was fond of Ginger. He went about everywhere with his dog, and played games with him when he came out of school. Ginger loved Terry too, and would have done anything in the world for him. His tail never stopped wagging when he was with Terry.

One day Terry was very excited. There was to be a grand garden party in the Rectory garden, with sweet-stalls, competitions, baby shows

and dog shows. Terry was going, and he made up his mind to buy some peppermint sweets and to have a bottle of ginger beer and two dips in the bran-tub.

"There's to be a maypole dance too," he told his mother, "and I shall watch that. Mr Jones is having a coconut shy, and I shall have two tries at that."

"Well, I will give you fifty pence to spend," said his mother. "That should be plenty for everything, Terry."

"Oh, thank you," said Terry. "I shall take Ginger with me and buy him a bar of chocolate. He'll love that."

When the day came Terry and Ginger walked to the garden party. Terry had the fifty pence piece in his pocket, and he was planning all he would do with it. He looked round the grounds and decided that he would start with a go at the coconut shy. He thought it would be lovely to win a big nut.

"I'll have a go," he said to the man. "How much?"

"Three balls for five pence," said the man. Terry put his hand into his pocket to get his money – and, oh dear me – it was gone! There was a hole at the bottom and the fifty-pence piece had dropped out!

Terry was so upset. He went back to look for his money but he couldn't find it anywhere. Ginger went with him and was just as upset as his master.

"Now I can't buy any sweets or ginger beer, or have any dips in the bran-tub," said poor Terry, sadly. "All my money is gone. Oh, Ginger, I do think it's bad luck, don't you?"

Ginger pushed his nose into Terry's hand and looked up at him with big brown eyes. He was very sorry for his master. He thought he would go and look for the lost money by himself, so he trotted off, nose to ground, trying to find the silver coin.

Suddenly Ginger came to where a great many dogs were all gathered together with their masters and mistresses, and he ran up to a collie dog called Rover, a great friend of his.

"What are you all doing here?" he asked Rover.

"Waiting for the dog shows," answered Rover.

"I hope you win a prize," said Ginger.

"Aren't you going in for the show?" asked Rover.

"No," said Ginger, wagging his tail. "My little master, Terry, is very sad. He has just lost all his money and I'm looking for it."

Just at that moment the dog show began, and the dogs moved into the ring. Ginger stayed to watch. It was a comic dog show, and there were prizes for the fattest dog, the thinnest dog, the dog with the saddest eyes, and the dog with the shortest legs. Ginger thought it was very funny.

"Now then!" cried the man who was running the dog show. "Which dog has the longest tail! Come along, everybody! I've got a measuring tape here to measure the tails with! Bring in your dogs! The one with the longest tail gets fifty pence!"

Now when Ginger heard that, a fine plan suddenly came into his head! Surely no dog had a longer tail than his! Everybody laughed at his tail because it was so very long. He would trot into the ring and show it to the judge!

So Ginger pushed his way through the people watching and trotted into the ring, where other dogs stood having their tails measured.

Ginger went right up to the judge and stuck his tail out to be measured.

"Ha!" cried the judge. "Here is a dog who thinks his tail is quite the longest! Stand still, Dog, and let me measure it!"

All the people laughed and Ginger stood quite still while the judge measured his tail.

"My goodness, what a long one!" he cried. "Why, it's two feet long! Little dog, I think you must have the prize! Who is the owner of this dog? Will he please step forward and take the prize?"

Now Terry happened to be peeping at the dog show at that moment and he was most astonished to see his dog, Ginger, trot into the ring and hold up his tail to be measured. He was still more surprised to hear that Ginger had won a prize, and he stepped into the ring to take it for him.

"Fifty pence!" said the judge, and he gave a nice bright silver coin to Terry. Then he patted Ginger and the grateful dog licked his hand.

"Good old Ginger!" said Terry, running off with him. "Fancy you thinking of putting yourself in for the longest-tailed dog! I know why you did it, Ginger! You did it because you were sorry that I had lost my money! You're the cleverest, dearest dog in the world, and I'm going to buy you a bun, two biscuits and a stick of chocolate!"

Ginger wagged his long tail and barked for joy. He bounded along by Terry and when his little master had bought him all that he had said he would, he wagged his long tail quite two hundred times a minute.

"Wuff, wuff!" he said, and he ate up the bun, the biscuits, and the chocolate in one gulp!

"Good old Ginger!" said Terry. "Now come along to the coconut shy! I'll see if I can't get a coconut *this* time!"

Off they went – and Terry knocked down the largest coconut of the lot! Wasn't he lucky? Then he went to buy some sweets and some ginger beer, and had three dips in the bran-tub – all with Ginger's fifty pence; and you may be sure there wasn't a prouder dog than Ginger at the garden party that day!

The lost baby mouse

There was once a little mouse who was far too daring. He ran out of his hole at any time of the day or night, and his mummy was very cross with him.

"One of these days you will get caught by the cat," she said.

"Oh, I'm too quick for the cat!" the little mouse said, and he twitched his whiskers to and fro in a way that made his mummy very angry.

"Don't make faces at me!" she cried, crossly. The little mouse gave a squeak and ran right out of his hole. Luckily for him the cat was not there, or that would have been the end of him. The hole led out into the kitchen, and there were often crumbs and scraps of food to

be found on the floor.

The little mouse hunted round for some, but there were none because the cook had swept them all up. "Well, I'll look round the world a bit and see what I can find somewhere else," thought the little mouse. So he ran out of the kitchen door into the hall.

He came to the stairs. He saw the first step – and the second step – and the third step – good gracious, it seemed to him as if these enormous stairs must lead up to the sky!

"Now I've heard that the moon is made of green cheese," said the baby mouse to himself, "and if so it would be a wonderful place to live. These great big steps must surely lead up to the moon. Tails and whiskers, how high up they go!"

The mouse began to climb them one by one. It seemed a very long way up to him. But at last he reached the very, very top. There was a landing at the top, and four or five doors led off it. The mouse ran into the nearest one.

It was the playroom where the children had all their toys, and played happily together. The mouse was very frightened to see a bear, a horse, a dog, an elephant, and a pink rabbit staring at him.

"Oh, pardon me!" he said, trying to back out of the door quickly. "I didn't know this was the zoo."

The teddy bear laughed so much that he couldn't speak. So the pink rabbit spoke up.

"Of course it's not the zoo, silly. We are only toys."

But the mouse had gone in a fright. He ran to another door. A bedroom was behind that, cold and empty. All the other doors were shut.

And then the cat appeared! My goodness! It came stalking round the corner of the landing, tail in air, green eyes gleaming!

The mouse gave a squeak of fright.

He ran into the playroom, with the cat after him. The cat pounced – and the baby mouse's tail was scratched with the cat's big claws. It dashed into an open brick-box and the teddy bear neatly shut the lid on him!

"Ssssss!" hissed the cat at the bear. But she didn't like his staring glass eyes and she turned and went out of the door again.

"She's gone," said the bear, opening the box. "Are you hurt, Baby Mouse?"

"My tail is bleeding," wept the poor little creature. "Oh, whatever am I to do? I am quite, quite lost. I was looking for the moon up here to have a good feast of green cheese – but it didn't seem to be anywhere."

"You won't find the moon up here, Baby Mouse. Hasn't your mummy ever told you about the playroom? We see her sometimes when the children take us downstairs," said the pink rabbit kindly. "I say, where's Angela the doll? She knows how to put bandages on.

Angela! Come over here and see to this dear little mouse."

Angela came up. She was a beautiful blue-eyed doll, with thick curly hair. She loved the tiny mouse as soon as she saw him. She made the pink rabbit fetch some water out of the goldfish bowl on the bookshelf to bathe the mouse's tail.

He climbed up with a dish out of the doll's house, and soon came back carrying the water very carefully.

"Good rabbit," said Angela. "Put the bowl down there. Get the sponge out of the doll's house bathroom."

There was the tiniest sponge imaginable in the bathroom, and the rabbit fetched it. Soon Angela was bathing the mouse's tail. Then she tore her tiny white handkerchief in half and bound it neatly round the little tail.

"Oh, thank you," said the mouse, gratefully. "I do think you are kind. What shall I do now? Is there a mouse hole anywhere in this playroom? I could go down it and live there. I shall never, never dare to go out of this room in case I meet the cat."

"Well, there isn't a mouse hole," said the pink rabbit. "We've often and often looked, little mouse. I suppose you wouldn't like to live in the brick-box?"

"No, thank you," said the mouse. "It's not very comfortable – and the children might tip me out with the bricks."

"True," said the bear. All the toys thought hard – and then the pink rabbit gave a squeal and clapped his fat paws together.

"I know!" he cried. "Why can't the baby mouse live in the doll's house? Nobody lives there at all, because the children took all the little dolls out to live in the toy farmyard and look after the animals there. The baby mouse is just small enough."

"Oh, that *is* a good idea!" cried everyone. "Come along, Mouse – we'll take you in at the front door."

So they all trooped across to the doll's house, and the teddy knocked on the little brass knocker. Of course there was nobody to answer, so they just pushed open the door. Only the mouse was small enough to go in at the door, and he ran into the tiny hall in delight.

"Oh, it's lovely!" he cried. "Really lovely! Look at the tiny stairs! Are there bedrooms above?"

"There is one bedroom and a tiny bathroom," said the rabbit, looking in at the window. "Here, Mouse, take the sponge and put it back again in the bathroom. And you can have a bath if you like."

Well, the baby mouse had a wonderful time. He filled the bath with water by turning on the tiny tap. He got into it and washed with the bit of soap there. He got out, stood on the teeny-weeny bath mat and dried himself with the towel. He did feel nice and clean after that.

"I feel dreadfully tired," he called to the toys, who were all peeping in at the windows, watching the mouse with joy. "Do you think I might sleep in this bed? It's just big enough for me. Would it matter if I got under the blankets do you think? I love to be cosy."

"Oh, *do* get into the bed!" cried the doll. "I will put my arm in at the window and tuck you up. You will look really sweet."

So the baby mouse got into the tiny doll's bed, and the big doll put her arm in through the open window and tucked him up. Just his ears, pointed nose, and whiskers showed above the sheet. He shut his eyes and in half a minute he was fast asleep.

All the toys came to peep at him, even the old plush monkey who was so bad-tempered that nobody liked playing with him. Everyone loved looking at the baby mouse asleep in the doll's tiny bed.

"He can live here as long as he likes," said Angela the doll. "He can have his meals in the kitchen off the little table. We will teach him good manners. He can keep the house clean, and sometimes, for a treat, he can cook us some tiny cakes on the stove. We've always wanted to use the doll's house stove, but we are all too big to go inside the kitchen door! Next time the children take me downstairs, I will tell his mummy that he is quite safe with us."

So the baby mouse lived in the doll's house, and felt quite safe there if the cat happened to come into the playroom. Once the cat came and looked in at the doll's house window, and the mouse sat on the kitchen table and made faces at her. Angela said he shouldn't have done that because it was bad manners.

"But I did so like making faces at the cat," said the mouse. "Really I did. Oh, toys, I'm so glad I came to your playroom. I do so love my little house. The only thing is – how I wish one of you was small enough to come and have tea with me!"

And now the little mouse has got his wish! A clockwork mouse has come to live with the toys – and today the real mouse is having the clockwork mouse to tea! Wouldn't you love to peep in at a window and see them both sitting in the kitchen together? I would!

The thrush and his anvil

It was a lovely spring morning. The birds were singing, and the sun shone into Jane's room so brightly that she woke up early and jumped out of bed without waiting for her mother to come and call her.

"I must go out and see how my plants are getting on," she thought. "We have had so many wet days lately that I have not been out in the garden for quite a long time. I'll go before breakfast, while it is fine."

She dressed quickly and ran out into the garden. The air smelt warm and moist after the rain. Jane had a little piece of garden of her own which she looked after with special care, and she hoped to find that her plants had grown quite big.

So they had, but, oh dear! nearly every leaf had a piece bitten off it! Jane was most upset. She ran round the rest of the garden, and found that Daddy's plants were just the same. Lots of his young lettuces were eaten too.

She rushed back to the house and burst into the dining room where Mummy, Daddy, and Peter were sitting down to breakfast.

"Daddy," she cried, "something is eating all our young plants! Something big too – not just a caterpillar or a grub."

"It's probably the snails," said Daddy. "After all, they have about fourteen thousand teeth on their tongues you know. They can do a lot of damage in one night! And there are generally a lot of them about after rain."

"Gracious – have snails got teeth on their tongues?" said Peter. "I never knew that. Fourteen thousand teeth –

why, their tongues must be like rasps, then!"

"They are," said Daddy, "like files. Of course, they are not the kind of teeth you and I have, Peter! But they are very strong, and a snail can eat most of a young plant in a night, using his ribbon-tongue."

"But doesn't he wear it out?" asked Jane.

"Yes, but it is always growing," said Daddy.

"Well, what are we to do about our snails?" asked Jane. "We can't let them eat everything in the garden. There must be dozens of them about."

"Finish your breakfast," said Daddy, "and then we will go and look at the damage."

They were soon out in the garden and looking at the plants.

Suddenly Daddy stopped and pointed to something.

"Hallo!" he said. "We needn't worry much about your plague of snails.

Somebody else knows about them and is dealing with them. See that stone? That is the thrush's anvil – the place he comes to when he has caught a snail and wants to smash its shell."

The children saw a flint beside the path. Round it were scattered many fragments of broken shell.

"Did the thrush really have the sense to come and use this stone for an anvil?" said Peter, half doubtful.

"Well, come into the summer-house here and we'll watch," said Daddy. "It's always better to see a thing for yourself than to hear about it second-hand. Come on."

They sat down in the summer-house and waited. They didn't have to wait long. Soon a thrush with a freckled breast flew down to the stone.

"He's got a snail in his beak!" whispered Jane.

So he had. Then he began to deal with the snail. He struck it hard on the stone anvil again and again.

Tap, tap, tap, tap! Tap, tap, tap, tap!

"I've often heard that noise before and I didn't know what it was!" whispered Peter. "Now I shall know it's a thrush using his anvil!"

The thrush worked hard. The snail-shell was strong and it wouldn't break. The thrush beat it down with all his might. Crack!

"It's broken!" said Jane. "Now he can get at the soft body inside. He's eating the snail, Daddy."

"Poor snail!" said Peter. "But he shouldn't eat our lettuces!"

"Clever thrush!" said Daddy, getting up. "Well – I think you can leave him to deal with your snails, don't you?"

Shellyback the tortoise

William and Susie had a tortoise. They called him Shellyback because his back was just a big hard shell, and they liked him very much. He wandered about all over the garden and ate the grass and any rose petals that he could find. He also ate some of Daddy's lettuces and some nice young pansy plants, which made Daddy very cross indeed.

Now, when Daddy had bought Shellyback, the man who was selling him had told Daddy that Shellyback would be most useful in the garden, and would eat up all the slugs and the beetles and caterpillars. So Daddy had been pleased, and was sure Shellyback

would be a good friend.

But tortoises eat green things, not insects, which they don't like at all, so Daddy found that Shellyback wasn't so useful in the garden after all. But, as Susie said, it wasn't poor Shellyback's fault that the man who had sold him told Daddy an untruth.

"I think we'll get rid of that tortoise," Daddy said when he found that some of his lettuces had been eaten. "He's no use at all."

"But, Daddy, we like Shellyback," said William. "Really, we do. He puts his head out of his shell when we come along and looks at us so nicely out of his little brown eyes. He is a friendly creature."

"Well, I'll give him another chance," said Daddy.

So Shellyback was allowed to wander about the garden again, and William and Susie watched to see that he did no damage. They got some wire and made him a little patch of grass of his own. They gave him a handful of rose petals, because he seemed to like those more than anything else. There old Shellyback lived in the sunshine, and seemed very happy indeed.

Then one autumn day he escaped and went into Daddy's seed-bed. Daddy had some nice young delphinium plants, all ready to plant out next year. He was very proud of them — and dear me,

Shellyback was very foolish indeed, for he chose just those to nibble right down to the ground.

When William and Susie got home from school they hunted for Shellyback, and when they found what he had done they were most alarmed.

"Daddy will certainly make us give him away now," said William. "Those delphiniums were his favourite plants. Oh, dear! Shellyback, you really are silly!"

The next day was Saturday. Daddy was going to spend it gardening. He went out happily into the garden and took his spade. It was good to be out in the sunshine even though the wind was frosty cold.

Daddy dug till he was tired, and then he went indoors to get his pipe. He put his hand into his pocket to get out his matches, and discovered that his key, which he kept in the same pocket, had gone. He must have dropped it whilst he was in the garden.

"Oh, bother!" said Daddy. "That's the key of the office safe. If I lose that it is a serious matter. I shan't be able to open the safe on Monday morning. William and Susie, you must help me to look for it in the garden."

"All right, Daddy," said William. "Where do you think you may have dropped it?"

"Anywhere, almost," said Daddy. "I've been nearly all over the garden this morning. The key may have fallen out of my pocket on to the path, or on the grass, or in the beds."

"Have you been in your young delphinium bed today?" asked Susie.

"No, why?" asked Daddy.

"Well, Daddy, we are sorry but Shellyback went there yesterday and ate your young plants." said Susie.

"What!" cried Daddy angrily. "He ate those lovely delphiniums of mine – the ones I grew from seed myself and have been watching so carefully all the summer? I said that tortoise must go and now he certainly must. He's a most destructive creature!"

Daddy jumped up and went striding out of doors to his young plants. When he saw his nice delphiniums nibbled right down to the roots he roared with rage.

"Where's that tortoise? I'll give him away to the milkman or the butcher or somebody this very day."

The children looked ready to cry. They knew that Shellyback certainly *would* go now.

"Go and fetch that tortoise and bring him here," said Daddy.

So off went William and Susie, but when they got to Shellyback's patch he wasn't there! He had pushed himself under the wire netting and had gone off somewhere.

They ran back to Daddy. "He's gone," they said.

"Gone?" said Daddy. "Well, he's probably eating something else of mine, then! Find him! And just hunt for my key at the same time."

The children hunted everywhere for Shellyback. They hunted under the bushes; they hunted under the hedge at the bottom of the garden; they even hunted indoors. But nowhere could the tortoise be seen. He had quite disappeared.

"Have you found him?" asked Daddy.

"No," said Susie. "We think he must have run away, Daddy. We've hunted everywhere."

"I expect he guessed he'd better make himself scarce," said Daddy. "Eating my plants like that! Now, help me to hunt for my key. I simply *must* find that."

Well, they hunted and they hunted for the key. But that key didn't seem to be anywhere in the garden. Like the tortoise, it had completely disappeared. Daddy was very upset.

"We must look again tomorrow," he said when the evening came and it was no use hunting any more. "I really must have it by Monday, or I may get into serious trouble at the office."

The children went to bed feeling sad. They didn't want Daddy to get into trouble, and they were unhappy because Shellyback had disappeared too. Things had gone very wrong that day!

The next day William and Susie went to the kitchen garden to see if there were any lettuces left for a salad. As they walked round it, they saw the place where Daddy had been digging the day before. The earth looked fresh and was dug very neatly, for Daddy was a good gardener.

As William looked along the earth, he saw something strange. He stopped and looked again.

"Susie," he said, "does it seem to you as if the earth is moving just over there? Look!"

He pointed, and Susie looked. She stared in surprise. The earth certainly *was* moving. It was just like a very tiny earthquake going on in one corner.

"How funny!" said Susie. "What can it be?"

"We'd better go and see," said William. So they ran to look. The earth was heaving here and there, and little bits came up into the air every now and again.

"It's some creature burying itself," said Susie. "Whatever is it?"

William fetched a spade, and very carefully dug all round the heaving earth. And then he saw what was burying itself. Guess what it was!

"It's Shellyback the tortoise!" cried Susie in astonishment. "He's burying himself. Oh, how funny! I didn't know tortoises buried themselves, did you, William? Had we better get him out, do you think?"

Just then their next-door neighbour, Miss White, looked over the wall, and they told her what was happening.

Miss White knew all about tortoises.

"Oh, yes," she said. "They always bury themselves in the ground in the winter because they don't like the cold, you know. They like to go to sleep all the winter through and wake up in the spring. If I were you I'd get him carefully out of the hole he has dug for himself and put him in a box of earth. If you leave him in the ground, Daddy may come along with his spade and crack his shell by accident when he digs over the bed. He will sleep in the box till the spring and wake up again then. Put him into a shed and he will be quite all right."

"I'm afraid Daddy is going to give him away," said Susie sadly. "But still, we'd better dig him up."

So, very carefully, the children took up old Shellyback – and as they wiped away the earth from his shell, something bright fell to the ground. William picked it up and stared at it in surprise.

"Daddy's key!" he cried. "Look, Susie,

it's Daddy's lost safe key! Oh, won't he
be pleased?"

"Shellyback found it!" said Susie.
"Shellyback found it! If it hadn't been
for him we wouldn't have seen it. It
would have lain in the ground for ever.
Come and tell Daddy."

Leaving the tortoise where he was, the children raced indoors to Daddy.

"Daddy! Daddy!" they shouted. "Here's your key! Look! It was in the bit of garden that you dug over yesterday. It must have fallen out when you were digging there."

Daddy was delighted. "Oh, good!" he said. "Thank you very much, children. I am so pleased to have my key again. I know how hard you have looked for it. I would like to give you a little reward. What would you like?"

Susie and William looked at each other. They both thought of the same thing – Shellyback!

"Daddy," said William, "*we* didn't find the key, really – Shellyback did!"

"Shellyback! But I thought he had gone," said Daddy. "You said you couldn't find him."

"He *had* gone," said Susie. "He had gone to bury himself for the cold winter, and the hole he dug up was where you had dropped your key, Daddy. So when we brushed the dirt off the tortoise, your key fell to the ground."

"Well, well, well!" said Daddy.

"So, Daddy, as Shellyback found your key for you, do you think you could let us still keep him?" asked William. "Miss White says he will sleep all through the winter in a box, so he won't do any more damage now – and we will promise to make his patch so strong with wire-netting next year that he can't possibly escape to eat your plants."

"Well, you seem to have made up your minds to keep Shellyback," said Daddy; "and as he really does seem to have found my key for me, I'll reward him – and you too. You may keep him."

"Oh, thank you, Daddy!" cried the two children, and they hugged Daddy hard.

Then they ran off to find a nice box for Shellyback. They put him in, with some earth at the bottom, and carried him in the box to the shed. They put him on a shelf there, and he is sleeping soundly, quite comfy and safe in his box.

I'd never have guessed it,
Brer Rabbit!

"Brer Rabbit," said Brer Terrapin, one day, hurrying in at the door. "Brer Rabbit, you'd better look out. Brer Fox and Brer Bear are after you!"

"That's nothing new!" said Brer Rabbit. "What's the matter with them now?"

"They say you charged them too much for sacks of carrots the other day," said Brer Terrapin. "They say they paid you far too much money."

"Well, they should have thought of that at the time," said Brer Rabbit. "I did charge them a good price – but after all I carried them all the way to their

homes for them."

"Yes, I know," said Brer Terrapin. "But you know what they are when they put their heads together and talk about you, Brer Rabbit. I tell you, they're coming after you and they're going to get their money back."

"Well, you sit at the front gate and just tell me when you see them coming," said Brer Rabbit. "I'm going to do a bit of cooking."

"*Cooking!* You'd better get busy and hide your money, hadn't you?" said Brer Terrapin, crawling out of the door.

"I'm just going to make a nice pie," said Brer Rabbit. "You go and keep watch for me, Brer Terrapin."

Soon Brer Rabbit was very busy. Brer Terrapin could see him through the open door. He saw him take down a pie-dish, and set out his pastry-board, and make pastry, rolling it flat. Well, well – to think Brer Rabbit could bother about cooking, when Brer Fox and Brer Bear would soon be along to search everywhere for their money!

He sat and watched the road, looking round every now and again to see what Brer Rabbit was doing. There now – he was putting the pastry on the pie-dish, and cutting it neatly round the edges, humming a little song all the time. And now he was putting the pie in the oven.

Then Brer Terrapin suddenly saw Brer Fox and Brer Bear pounding along the road at top speed. He called out at once. "Here they come, Brer Rabbit, a-panting and a-blowing, here they come!"

He crawled behind the wall, just as the two crashed in at the gateway, both as angry as could be. "Hey, Brer Rabbit, you know what *we've* come for, don't you?" growled Brer Bear, bursting in at Brer Rabbit's front door.

"To join me in a nice juicy pie?" said Brer Rabbit. "I've just this minute finished making one. It will be cooked soon – do stay and have some."

"Pies! We haven't come for PIES!" raged Brer Fox, and began to open drawers and cupboards. "*You* know what we've come for – to get back our money! You charged us double the price for those carrots, you cheat of a rabbit!"

"Well, didn't I carry them all the way home for you?" said Brer Rabbit. "Didn't I now? That made them worth double, didn't it?"

"I'm not going to argue with you, Brer Rabbit," said Brer Fox, looking under the bed. "All I want is that money! Yes, and we'll take ALL of it, not just half. That will teach you to cheat us!"

What a mess the two of them made of poor Brer Rabbit's house! They tore the blankets off the bed, they emptied pails and brushes out of the cupboard, they threw things out of every drawer — but they couldn't find any money at all, except for six pennies in an old brown teapot on the mantelpiece!

Brer Terrapin trembled at the front gate. Good gracious, what a mess Brer

268

Rabbit's house was in! And what would happen when Brer Fox and Brer Bear at last found the money? It was hidden *somewhere*, Brer Terrapin was quite certain of that!

Brer Fox and Brer Bear had to give up the hunt a last. They pocketed the six pennies, and that was all they found! They stamped out of the house angrily, shaking their fists at Brer Rabbit.

"All right! So the money isn't hidden in your house! We're at least sure of that! Tomorrow we'll come back and dig up the garden! And don't *you* start digging it yourself! We're going to set little Jack Sparrow to watch you, and he'll tell us just as soon as he sees you turning up any earth in your garden!"

"Oh, don't leave in such a temper," begged Brer Rabbit. "I've a pie cooking in the oven – you saw it yourself when you peeped in. Have dinner with me just to show you're friendly."

"We're NOT friendly," barked Brer Fox, and went out of the gate with Brer

Bear, slamming it so hard that it almost broke.

"Why did you ask them to stay for dinner?" said Brer Terrapin, crawling into the kitchen. "It was a silly thing to do, Brer Rabbit. They've done enough damage as it is."

"Oh, we'll soon clear that up!" said Brer Rabbit, cheerfully. "Put the cheese on the table, Brer Terrapin, and the bread, and I'll go and pick some lettuces."

Soon they were sitting having cheese and lettuce, and very nice it was, too. "What about the pie?" said Brer Terrapin. "Not that I can eat very much more!"

Brer Rabbit fetched the pie out of the oven and set it on the table. The crust was very nicely browned. Brer Rabbit took a knife and cut two pieces of crust, setting a piece on each plate. "What sort of pie is it?" asked Brer Terrapin.

"It's a *clinky-clink* pie," said Brer Rabbit, solemnly. "One of my *special* pies!" He ladled out some on a spoon, and Brer Terrapin was surprised to hear a loud clinking noise.

"Brer Rabbit! Brer RABBIT! You've cooked *money* inside this dish!" he cried. "Look at it – money! So THAT'S where you hid your money – in the pie!"

"Yes," said Brer Rabbit, eating the crust. "And don't say I wasn't hospitable to Brer Fox and Brer Bear – I asked them to stay to dinner and *share* the pie, didn't I? But they were rude and said no. Ah well – they *could* have shared the money if they'd wanted to! I'd have ladled it out on to their plates, and laughed to see their faces."

"A *clinky-clink* pie!" said Brer Terrapin, staring at the money on his plate. "Brer Rabbit, whatever will you think of next? What a hiding-place to be sure! I'd never have guessed it, never."

Nor would I, Brer Terrapin, nor would I!

Brer Bear's party

Once Brer Bear, Brer Wolf and Brer Fox got together and said they'd have a party, and ask Brer Rabbit too.

"You see, Brer Bear, you don't need to get any dinner ready for us if you ask old Brer Rabbit," grinned Brer Fox. "All you'll want will be three plates, three knives and forks, and one good big pot of boiling water ready on the fire!"

"All right," said Brer Bear. "I don't feel very friendly towards Brer Rabbit just now. He's always making fun of me and tricking me. I'm just about tired of him."

"Now don't you tell him that you've asked me and Brer Wolf," said Brer Fox.

"Just ask him in to dinner tomorrow, and tell him you've got something special for him. Say you've got hot chestnut-pie. He loves chestnuts."

"You leave it to me. I'll manage Brer Rabbit all right!" said Brer Bear. So he went out to find old Brer Rabbit.

He came to Brer Rabbit's house and knocked on the door, blim-blam, blim-blam!

"Who's there?" asked Brer Rabbit.

"A good friend of yours!" shouted back Brer Bear.

"Good friends ask people out to dinner!" yelled back Brer Rabbit.

"Well, that's just what I've come to ask you!" said Brer Bear. "You come along to dinner with me tomorrow, Brer Rabbit, and I'll have a nice hot chestnut-pie for you!"

Brer Rabbit was astonished to hear such a thing from Brer Bear. He poked his head out of the window and stared at him hard. Brer Bear stared back, and didn't blink an eyelid.

"All right, I'll be along," said Brer Rabbit, and popped his head in again.

Now the more Brer Rabbit thought about Brer Bear, the funnier he thought it was that Brer Bear should ask him to dinner.

"But I'll go," said Brer Rabbit to himself. "Oh yes, I'll go – and I'll come back too, though maybe Brer Bear isn't expecting me to!"

Twelve o'clock was Brer Bear's dinner-time. Brer Rabbit scuttled along to his house at half-past eleven, just to see what he could see. All he saw from outside was a mighty lot of smoke coming from Brer Bear's chimney.

"That's a mighty big fire to cook a small chestnut-pie!" said Brer Rabbit, rubbing his chin. "I'll just look in at the window and see what I can see."

So he peeped in, and all he saw was an enormous pot boiling on a big fire, and, on the table, three plates and three knives and forks. Nothing else at all.

"Funny!" said Brer Rabbit. "*Three* plates! I don't like it. No, I don't like it."

He couldn't see anyone in the room at all. Brer Wolf and Brer Fox were hidden behind a curtain, and Brer Bear was waiting by the door.

"Shall I go and knock at the door or not?" wondered Brer Rabbit. "Yes – I'll go – but Brer Bear won't get me indoors. No – I'll take him for a walk that he won't like!"

So Brer Rabbit marched round to the door and knocked loudly on it – BLAM, BLAM, BLAM!

Brer Bear opened it at once, and grinned all over his big mouth.

"Come along in," he said. "The pie is cooking."

"Well, Brer Bear, I hope you've got shrimp sauce with it," said Brer Rabbit, not going indoors. "I surely hope you have. You know, chestnut-pie is nothing without shrimp sauce."

"Well, no, I haven't got shrimp sauce," said Brer Bear. "But you come along in and taste the pie, Brer Rabbit. You won't want shrimp sauce, I know you won't."

"Oh yes, I shall," said Brer Rabbit. "And what's more, I'm not going to eat the pie without shrimp sauce, Brer Bear. If only I'd known you'd got no shrimp sauce, I'd have brought you along a whole heap of shrimps myself. There's plenty in the old well not far from here."

"I thought shrimps were only found in the sea," said Brer Bear, astonished.

"Not the sort of shrimps *I'm* talking about!" said Brer Rabbit.

"Well, never mind about shrimps," said Brer Bear, hearing an impatient noise from behind the curtains. "You come in and smell the pie, Brer Rabbit. If you don't like it, you can go."

"I tell you I'm not going to eat any pie without hot shrimp sauce," said Brer Rabbit. "I'll tell you what, Brer Bear! You get your net and come along with me to the well and fish up a few shrimps. I can't reach down, I'm too short, but you could easily reach with a net."

"Oh, all right, all right!" said Brer Bear. He went indoors and found his net.

A loud whisper came from behind the curtains: "Don't you let Brer Rabbit out of your sight, Brer Bear! Get the shrimps and bring him back at once."

"All right, all right," said Brer Bear, who was beginning to feel that he was doing all the work. He went out of the house and slammed the door. Then he and Brer Rabbit set off together.

"You see, Brer Bear, nobody who is anybody ever dreams of eating chestnut-pie without shrimp sauce," said Brer Rabbit as they went along. "I'm really surprised that you didn't think of it."

"Oh, you are, are you," said Brer Bear, feeling more and more annoyed. "Well, we'll get the silly shrimps and make them into sauce – though I guess you've got enough sauce of your own without bothering about any extra, Brer Rabbit!"

They came to the well. Brer Bear looked down into the deep, dark water. He couldn't see a single shrimp, and this was not really surprising, because there wasn't one to see!

"Ah, look! There goes a shrimp – and another – and another!" said Brer Rabbit in an excited voice. "Oooh, look at that fat fellow. Isn't he a lovely red colour!"

"I thought shrimps didn't go red till they were cooked," said Brer Bear, surprised.

"These shrimps are not like the ones you've seen before," said Brer Rabbit firmly. "Quick, Brer Bear – catch them, catch them! Put in your net!"

Brer Bear put in his net, hoping that a few shrimps would swim into it, for he couldn't see a single one to catch. But his net wouldn't quite reach.

"Lean right over, lean right over!" cried Brer Rabbit. "Then your net will reach!"

"Well, hold on to my trousers then," said Brer Bear.

So Brer Rabbit caught hold of the seat of Brer Bear's trousers, and Brer Bear leaned right over to make his net reach the water.

And then suddenly Brer Rabbit let go of Brer Bear's trousers – and down he went into the well, splish, splash!

"Oooble, oooble, ooble," gurgled poor Brer Bear, spluttering and choking as he came up again, and floundered about in the water. "Brer Rabbit, you let me go! And just look here – there isn't a single shrimp to be seen! They're not real!"

"They're just as real as your chestnut-pie, Brer Bear!" grinned Brer Rabbit, learning over the top of the well. "Yes, just as real! Goodbye! I hope you enjoy your bathe!"

He skipped off back to Brer Bear's house, dancing as he went. He poked his head in at the door and yelled to Brer Wolf and Brer Fox:

"Heyo, there! Brer Bear says there are such a lot of shrimps down that well, he wants some help. Hurry along, hurry along!"

Brer Fox and Brer Wolf rushed to the well to get some of the shrimps, but all they saw there was a very wet, very cold, and very angry bear!

"Get him out and give him some of that hot chestnut-pie!" yelled Brer Rabbit, dancing about in the distance. "He can have my share – and tell him he can have sauce from Brer Rabbit, instead of from shrimps! He'll like that, he will!"

And off went Brer Rabbit in delight, stopping every now and again to roll on the ground and laugh like twenty hyenas!

The six fairy dolls

In the toyshop sat six fairy dolls. They were all sizes. The biggest was nearly two feet high, and very lovely. The next was smaller, and the third and fourth were pretty little dolls with silvery wings. The fifth one was only six inches high, but she was beautifully dressed, and carried a silver wand.

The last one was very tiny, and stood no higher than a child's little finger. Her wings were only silver paper, and her wand was a bit of wire. Her dress was the tiniest bit of muslin, and her feet were so small that she wore no shoes at all.

The big dolls talked together, and didn't take any notice of the tiny fairy

doll. She listened to them, and wished she was as big as they were.

"We are sure to be bought for a Christmas party," said one fairy doll. "I am the biggest, so I expect I shall be chosen first. I shall be put right at the top of a big Christmas tree, and I shall be able to look down and see everything."

"I am nearly as big as you," said the second. "I expect I shall be bought too. I would do nicely for a smaller Christmas tree."

"We are very pretty little dolls," said the third and fourth. "We heard the shopkeeper say so when she put us in the window. She said we were sure to sell."

"I am the prettiest of you all," said the fifth. "I have the loveliest dress – it is all made by hand – and my wand glitters just like silver! I am very grand. I expect I shall be bought by a very rich lady for her children's tree. I shall go first, I am sure."

"What about me?" asked the tiniest doll. "Shall I be bought too?"

"Pooh, you!" said all the other dolls at once. "There's no Christmas tree small enough for you! You'll never be sold. You'll just stay on the shelf for years, and then get so dirty that you'll have to be thrown away."

The days went past, and Christmas came near. No one came to buy any of the fairy dolls at all. They were very much disappointed. At last Christmas Eve came, and just as the shopkeeper was going to close the shop for the night, the shop bell tinkled.

All the fairy dolls sat up straight. Perhaps someone was going to buy them at last! It was a little old woman, and she looked across to the fairy dolls.

"I want a fairy doll, please," she said. The shopkeeper fetched them all and sat them on the counter.

"How lovely they are!" said the little old woman. "But most of them are much too big. I want just a little tiny one to put on a Christmas cake."

"Then this one would be just right," said the shopkeeper, and she took up the tiniest doll of all. How proud and pleased she was!

"Yes, that one will do nicely!" said the old woman. She put a ten pence piece down on the counter, and the shopkeeper wrapped the little doll in brown paper. All the other dolls stared in dismay. The tiny doll had been bought first, after all. No one had wanted *them*! What a disappointment!

"We'd better not be so proud of ourselves next Christmas!" whispered the biggest fairy doll, as the shopkeeper packed them away in boxes for the next year. "I wonder what that tiny little doll is doing now?"

Ah, she was having a fine time! She had been put right in the very middle of a beautiful Christmas cake. Round her were little brown bunnies and little red gnomes made of marzipan. They thought the fairy doll was the most beautiful thing they had ever seen.

"You shall be our little queen!" they said. And at midnight they crowned her, and danced round her in a ring. How happy she was! When tea-time came on Christmas Day everyone admired her, and all the children said how sweet she was. They begged their mother to be careful not to cut her when she cut the cake.

And what became of her after the party? Well, she was put into the dolls' house to look after it! She is just the right size, and you may be sure she keeps the house beautifully! There isn't a speck of dust anywhere. She sleeps in the little bed there every night, and is as happy as a lark in spring-time. You should just hear her singing when she cooks her breakfast on the little tin stove in the dolls' house kitchen!

The tale of a tail

A most exciting letter had come from the brownies in the wood to the toys in Michael's playroom. This is what it said.

"Dear Animals,
We are holding a party for all toy animals in the woods at midnight tomorrow. Please come.
Love from
The Brownies.
PS – By animals we mean those with tails."

"Oh! A party in the woods just for toy animals! What a wonderful idea," said the clockwork mouse.

"I shall wear my best blue bow," said the pink cat.

"I shall put a special wag in my tail," said the black dog.

"I shall practise climbing so that I can climb the trees," said the monkey.

"And I shall make sure my growl is in good order, so that I can make the brownies laugh," said the teddy bear.

The pink cat looked at him. "You can't go to the party," she said.

"Don't be silly," said the bear. "Of course I can go. I'm an animal! Bears are always animals."

"Yes, but you haven't got a tail," said the pink cat. "You saw what it said in the note. 'By animals we mean those with tails.'"

The bear stared behind him in alarm. "Haven't I got a tail?" he said. "Why haven't I got a tail?"

"I don't know, I don't believe teddy bears ever have tails," said the pink cat. "Anyway, you can't go. It plainly says that only those with tails can go."

"But it didn't mean *I* can't go," said the bear. "Why, everyone knows I'm an animal! I can't help it if I haven't got a tail. It just means that people like the baby doll or the sailor doll can't go. It doesn't mean bears."

"Well, I'm sure it *does*," said the black dog. "They think you're a toy, like the baby doll. They don't count you as an animal. You can't possibly go, Teddy. They might turn you back."

The bear began to cry. He did like parties so very much. "Oh, don't go without me! I couldn't bear it," he sobbed. "Please, please let me go with you. Don't go without me."

The toys were sorry for him. He was a nice bear, kind and jolly. It was a shame he couldn't go because he had no tail.

Then the monkey had an idea. "I know! Can't he get a tail? Then he could go!"

"Oh, yes, oh, yes! I'll get a tail!" cried the bear, and wiped his eyes at once. He gave the monkey a hug. "How kind of you to think of such a good idea! Where can I get a tail?"

Nobody knew. Then the black dog remembered something he had heard Michael say. Michael was the little boy who lived in the house and played with the toys.

"I once heard Michael say that his favourite tail was in that book over there," he said, and he pointed to a book on the bookshelf. The toys stared in surprise.

"I didn't know Michael had a tail," said the bear.

"He hasn't," said the toy boat. "I swim in the bath with him, and I know he hasn't got a tail. He has a dear little pink fat body, but no tail."

"Well, he keeps it in that book, I tell you," said the black dog. "He must have two or three tails, and that is his favourite one, the one in the book."

"Are you *sure* you heard him say his favourite tail was in the book?" said the monkey.

"Yes. Quite, quite sure," said the black dog, impatiently. "I've got two good ears, haven't I?"

"Well, then, we've only got to look through the book and borrow the tail when we find it," said the pink cat. "I should think it would be a bit squashed, but that won't matter."

So they got the book down and began to hunt through it. But they couldn't find any tail at all. And this wasn't surprising, because what Michael had meant, of course, was that his favourite story or *tale* was in that book — but the black dog had quite thought he meant a waggy tail, like the one he wore himself.

It was very disappointing. There was no tail there at all. They turned all the pages over again very carefully. Still no tail.

"Michael must have taken it out," said the monkey. The bear looked very sad. He rubbed his paw over his eyes, and the curly-haired doll gave him her hanky.

"Don't cry," she said. "Maybe Michael has put it somewhere else. We'll look."

But they couldn't find a tail anywhere, of course. The bear was very sad that night, and very sad all the next day.

When the night of the party came he was sadder still. It would be dreadful to watch the toys going off to the party without him. If only, only he had a tail.

Then he would be counted as an animal.

"Shall we set the musical box going, just to practise a dance or two before we go?" said the monkey. "I've rather forgotten my dance steps."

So they set the musical box going, and began to dance. The bear stood near, watching sadly. If only he was going to dance at a party too!

The toys had forgotten to shut the door, and Michael awoke when he heard the music from the musical box. He sat up in bed in surprise. Who was playing the musical box in the middle of the night?

He jumped out of bed to see. He put his head in at the playroom door, and watched the toy animals dancing together. The monkey danced with the dog. The cat danced with the toy horse. The donkey danced with the mouse. The rabbit danced with the little toy lamb.

Only the bear didn't dance. He stood near the door, his back to Michael, and tears ran down his face. He turned away to hide them – and Michael saw that his dear old teddy was crying.

"What's the matter?" he said to the bear, and all the toys and animals jumped in great surprise. They shot back into the toy cupboard at top speed. Only the bear stayed where he was, and looked at Michael.

"Why are you crying, Teddy?" said Michael, and picked up the fat, little bear. "I've never seen you cry before. I didn't know you could."

"Michael – you said your favourite tail was in that book, but it isn't," said the bear. "Where do you keep your tails? Could you lend me one?"

Michael couldn't understand at first. Then he guessed the funny mistake that the bear had made and he laughed. "You've muddled up what I meant!" he said. "I meant that my favourite story was in that book, silly! I have no tail – not the sort that grow on you."

"Oh, dear," said the bear, sadly. "I see.

So you can't lend me one. And I can't possibly go to the party."

"What party?" asked Michael, surprised. The bear told him all about it.

"Well, fancy saying that only animals with tails can go! I'm sure that's a mistake," said Michael. "But never mind – let's see what I can find for you in the way of a tail. I'm sure I can think of something."

He remembered an old hat of his mother's. It had a little tail of white fur in front. He could take that off and sew it on the bear! That would make a most wonderful tail for him.

Michael went to find the old hat. It was in a box in the chest on the landing. Mother had often said she didn't think she could ever wear it again. Michael took it out – and there was the little white tail, just as he remembered it. Good!

He ripped it off. Then he found a needle and cotton in his mother's work-basket and he threaded the needle.

"Shall I hurt you if I sew this on your back?" he asked the bear.

"Oh no," said the bear. "What a simply lovely tail! It looks so real! Shall I be able to wag it?"

"I don't know," said Michael, feeling rather doubtful. "It hasn't a wag in it at the moment. Now, keep still. It doesn't match your brown fur, but never mind!"

He sewed the white tail firmly on to the bear's back. He broke off the cotton and gave the bear a little push. "There you are! Turn round and show the others. You look really fine!"

The bear was so proud that he couldn't stand still. He strutted up and down, showing off his grand white tail. It was a bit big for him and didn't match. But he was so very happy about it. His happiness suddenly got into the tail, and it began to swing about.

"It's got a wag! Look, it's got a wag!" said the bear, happily, and he swung his new tail so well that he hit the clockwork mouse on the nose.

"It's time to start," said the black cat, as he heard the clock in the hall strike a quarter to twelve. "Goodbye, Michael. Thank you for your help."

"Have a nice time!" said Michael, and went back to bed, delighted at his little midnight adventure.

The animals all set off to the party. The bear didn't feel a bit afraid of being turned back now that he had a tail. He swung it about all the time.

To his surprise there were other teddy bears there – without tails! The brownies explained their mistake, and welcomed all the bears that came.

"We forgot that teddy bears didn't have tails. We are so glad you came."

"*Well*! I needn't have gone to all this bother of getting myself a tail after all!" said the bear, feeling rather cross.

But he didn't feel cross for long. You see, there was a special prize offered for the best tail – and the teddy bear won it! His was such a big and surprising tail that everyone voted it was the very best one. So he got the prize.

It was a fine prize. It was a box of chocolates – and each chocolate was a little brown bear! Wasn't that lovely? The bear ate one and handed the box round.

"I must keep a few for Michael," he thought. "I really must." So he did. He put them on Michael's pillow, and Michael found them in the morning.

"I suppose the bear brought them home for me from the party," thought Michael, eating them. "How kind of him! I must take his tail off today and put it back on Mummy's hat."

But the bear didn't want to part with his beautiful new tail, so Michael asked his mother if she minded him keeping the tail off her old hat. She didn't, so Michael let the bear keep it.

He still wears it, so you will know him if you ever see him. He must be the only teddy bear in the world with a tail!

It's Christmas time

"It's Christmas time!" said the big rocking-horse in the toy shop, one night when the shop was shut, and only the light of the street lamp outside lit up the toys sitting on the shelves and counters.

"What's Christmas?" asked a small bear who had only just come.

"Oh, it's a lovely time for children," said the horse, rocking gently to and fro. "They have presents, you know, and Father Christmas comes on Christmas night and fills their stockings with all kinds of toys."

"*You'll* never go into a stocking, rocking-horse!" said a cheeky monkey.

"No, I shall stand in somebody's

playroom and give children rides," said the horse. "I *shall* look forward to that. I've been here a long time – too long. But I'm very expensive, you know, and people often haven't enough money to buy me."

"I should like to be sold and go to live with children who would love me and play with me," said the fat teddy bear. "I shall growl for them – listen – urrrrrrrr-rrrrr!"

"Don't!" said the little furry rabbit sitting next to him. "You frighten me when you do that. I think you're going to bite me."

"Don't worry. You know he wouldn't," said the big sailor doll, leaning down from the shelf above. "Come on, Bunny – let's get down to the floor and have a game!"

The rabbit jumped down at once, and the big sailor doll landed near him. He loved the sailor, who wouldn't let any of the bigger toys tease him or frighten him. Sometimes the pink cat chased him and the little rabbit couldn't bear that!

"Sailor," said the rabbit, when all the toys were playing together, "Sailor, we're friends, aren't we? Sailor, you won't leave me if you are sold and go to live with some children, will you?"

"Well – I shan't be able to help it," said Sailor. "You're my very best friend and I'm yours, and I hope and hope we'll be sold together – but you never know!"

The bunny worried about that, and next day when customers came in and out of the shop, buying this toy and that, the little rabbit hoped that he and the sailor doll would be bought by the same person.

But they weren't! A little old woman came in and asked for a sailor doll for her grand-daughter whose father was a sailor – and the shop lady at once took down Sailor from his shelf.

"He's fine," said the little old woman. "Yes, I'll have him. My grand-daughter Mary will love him! Will you wrap him up for me, please?"

"Goodbye, Sailor!" whispered the little rabbit. "Oh, I shall miss you so! Goodbye, and be happy!"

Sailor only had time to wave before he was wrapped up in brown paper. Then he was carried out of the shop by the old woman, and Bunny was left by himself. He felt lonely and unhappy, and he hoped that the bear wouldn't growl at him or the pink cat chase him.

But he was sold that very day too! A big, smiling woman came in and bought a great many toys at once.

"They're for a Christmas tree," she said. "I am giving a party on Boxing Day for my little girl and her friends, and we've got a perfectly lovely tree."

"You'll want a fairy doll for the top, then," said the shop lady, pleased. "And what about a little bear and a doll or two?"

"Yes. And I'll have that ship – and that wooden engine – and that top," said the customer. "And I really *must* have that little rabbit – he's sweet!"

Bunny was sold! He couldn't believe it. He was sold at last and would leave the toy shop he knew so well. He was glad he was going with so many other toys he knew – but oh dear, each of them would be given to a different child, so he wouldn't have any friends at all after Boxing Day!

The toys were excited. It was fun to be sold and to go out to some family. It would be fun to hang on a Christmas tree and have crowds of children admiring them. It would be simply lovely if they were lucky enough to belong to a kind and loving child who would play with them and perhaps even cuddle them in bed.

Bunny was surprised to see such a big Christmas tree. It almost reached the ceiling! "I don't think I want to be hung up there," he said to the big teddy bear, who had been sold for the tree too. "I might fall off."

"Don't be silly," said the bear. "Ah – here comes someone to see to us! Cheer up, you silly little rabbit, and if you are given to some horrid child, well, just run away!"

"Where to?" asked the rabbit, anxiously, but the bear was very busy growling at that moment, because someone was pressing him in the middle where his growl was kept!

"Urrrr!" he said proudly. "Urrrr!"

The rabbit was hung high up on the tree, and dangled to and fro there. He didn't like it. The ground seemed so far away! All the other toys hung there too, and pretty fairylights shone brightly in red, blue, yellow and green from the top of the tree to the bottom.

"The party's tonight!" said a doll next to him. "Not long to wait now! Doesn't the fairy doll look wonderful at the top of the tree?"

Soon the rabbit heard the sound of children's voices and laughter. They were playing games in another room.

Then someone came quickly into the big room where the tree stood and switched on all the fairylights again. The tree glowed and shone, and all the pretty ornaments on it glittered brightly. The toys looked lovely as they hung there.

How the children cheered and clapped when they came running in and saw the lovely tree. "It's beautiful!" they shouted. "Oh, look at the toys! Oh, the fairy doll! Wave your wand, fairy doll, and do some magic!"

"Now, there is a toy for everyone," said the lady who was giving the party. "Harry, here is a ship for you," and she gave him the ship. "Lucy, here is a doll. I know you want one. Molly, here is a bear with a growl."

The little rabbit looked down on the children. Was there a little girl called Mary there? The sailor doll had been bought for a Mary. Oh, wouldn't it be wonderful if he was given to a girl called Mary, the one who had Sailor?

Who was Bunny going to? He looked and looked at the children. He did hope somebody kind would have him – a nice little girl, perhaps, with a merry face.

"And now, what about a present for *you*, Peter," said the kind lady at the tree. "You're not very old – I think you shall have this little furry bunny. Here you are!"

So Bunny went to Peter, who held him very tight indeed, and squeezed him to see if he had a squeak inside. But he hadn't. Bunny didn't like Peter very much, especially when he dropped him on the floor and somebody nearly trod on him.

"Be careful of your little rabbit, Peter," said a big girl.

"I don't like him," said Peter. "I wanted that engine."

The rabbit wondered if he could run away. He didn't want to go home with Peter. He was sure he was one of the horrid children he had heard spoken about in the toy shop.

But he did go home with Peter, and with him went a jigsaw puzzle for Peter's sister.

"Give this to your sister, Peter," said somebody. "It is such a pity she's in bed with a cold and can't come. This jigsaw shall be her present."

Peter carried the rabbit and the jigsaw home. As soon as he got there he went up to his sister's bedroom. She was in bed, with a large hanky under her pillow.

"Look – they sent you a jigsaw," said Peter. "And I got this silly little rabbit. I'd much rather have the jigsaw!"

"Oh, Peter – he's sweet!" said the little girl in bed. "I've so many jigsaws – you take that one and I'll have the bunny. He shall come into bed with me, he looks rather lonely. He's only a baby one!"

"All right. I'd like the jigsaw," said Peter. He threw the rabbit to his sister and went out with the jigsaw. The little girl took the rabbit and looked at him. "Yes, I like you," she said. "You shall sleep with me at night, so long as you don't mind sharing my bed with another toy. Look, here he is – my very best new toy!"

She pulled back the sheet – and Bunny stared as if he couldn't believe his eyes. Who do you suppose was cuddled down in bed, looking very happy? Why, Sailor! Yes, it was the big sailor doll, the one from the toy shop, Bunny's own special friend. Sailor almost sat up in surprise, but just remembered not to. He smiled, though, he smiled and smiled!

"I think you like each other," said Mary, because that was her name, of course! "Yes, I'm sure you do. I hope so, anyway, because you've just *got* to be friends. You see, you will sit together on my bed each day, and cuddle down with me at night!" She put Bunny beside Sailor, and lay down. She closed her eyes, and was soon asleep. And then – what a whispering there was beside her!

"*You!*" said Sailor, in delight. "What a bit of luck!"

"*You!*" said Bunny. "Oh, I can't believe it! What's Mary like?"

"Fine," said Sailor. "You'll love her. Oh, Bun – what lovely times we're going to have! You'll like the other toys here, too, all except a rude monkey – but I won't let him tease you! Fancy, we shall be able to be friends all our lives now!"

That was three years ago – and they are still with Mary, though they don't sleep with her at night now, because she thinks she's too big for that. "It *is* nice to have a friend," Bun keeps saying. Well, it is, isn't it?

Magic in the playroom

The toys in the playroom were very friendly with the little folk who lived in the garden. There were fairies and pixies, gnomes and brownies, all merry and happy and friendly. Sometimes it was the gnomes who came to drink a cup of tea in the dolls' house. Sometimes it was the pixies who came to dance to the music of the little musical box. And sometimes it was the fairies or the brownies who came to play at hide-and-seek with the toys.

They did have fun, and the toys always loved to see the pretty heads of the little folk peeping over the windowsill. But when a family of goblins came to live in the old oak tree in the garden the toys were not quite so pleased to see them.

"The goblins are not so polite as the fairies," said the pink rabbit, shaking his head.

"The goblins have rather bad

313

manners," said the big doll.

"They make a noise when they eat," said the red-haired doll, who was very particular indeed.

But nobody said anything rude to the goblins, and each night they popped in at the window with the other little folk.

Then a horrid thing happened. One night, after the little folk had gone back to the garden, the pink rabbit put his hand up to his collar and found that the little brooch which kept his coat together at the neck was quite gone!

"I believe I saw it peeping out of the pocket of one of the goblins," said the clockwork mouse suddenly.

There was a deep silence. The toys were too shocked for words. To think that one of their guests would steal something!

"You must be wrong, Mouse," said the pink rabbit at last. "My brooch must have dropped somewhere."

So they hunted for it, but it could not

be found. "We will not say anything about it at all," said the rabbit. "It is horrid to think that anyone would steal from us."

But after that other things began to go! The red-haired doll missed her necklace! She usually kept it in the kitchen cupboard in the dolls' house, because she was so afraid of losing it – and one night when she went to put it on, it was not in the cupboard! Oh dear!

And worse than that, the walking duck lost her key! It was always kept on a ribbon, tied to her neck, so that it should not be lost. It was easy to wind up the walking duck when she had her key handy like that. But now it was gone! Someone had cut her ribbon in half and taken the key, perhaps when she was playing a game and was too excited to notice.

The toys stared at one another in dismay. Something really *must* be done now! There was no doubt at all that those bad-tempered little goblins had taken their things.

"We will complain to the others," said the walking duck. "Surely the fairies, the pixies, the brownies, and the gnomes will be able to make the goblins give back to us all the things they have stolen!"

So that night the rabbit took Ringding the fairy, Twinks the pixie, Frisk the brownie, and Snip the gnome into the kitchen of the dolls' house and shut the door.

"Whatever is the matter?" asked Ringding in alarm, looking at the rabbit's solemn pink face. "You look as if you have lost a new penny and found a broken button!"

"I've something to tell you," said the rabbit, "and I don't want the goblins to hear me. Little folk, I am sorry to say that the goblins have been stealing some of our things."

The little folk stared at the pink rabbit in horror. Could it really be true? Ringding went very red indeed. She felt quite cross.

"I don't believe it," she said. "You have made a mistake, Rabbit."

But when the rabbit told her about his brooch and the red-haired doll's necklace and the walking duck's key, the little folk nodded their heads.

"Yes," said Twinks the pixie. "I believe you, Rabbit. It was only yesterday that I noticed the goblins had a new front door key fitting their lock in the oak tree — and now I come to think of it, it was exactly like the key belonging to the walking duck!"

"What shall we do about it?" said Frisk the brownie.

"We shall have to use some magic on the goblins," said Snip the gnome. "We must make them give up the stolen things somehow."

"But the goblins know more magic than we do," said Ringding. "Whatever spell we do to make them give back what they have stolen will be of no use

– for the goblins know much stronger spells than we do!"

"Well, we will try, anyway," said Snip.

So that night, when the goblins had all gone from the playroom into the garden, the little folk went to the oak tree where the goblin family lived and made a spell to force them to give up the stolen goods. But it was no use at all! The goblins put their heads out of their little window and laughed at them.

"You don't know enough magic!" they shouted. "Stop your silly spells, or we will make a stronger one and turn you into ladybirds!"

The little folk went away. They didn't want to be turned into ladybirds! They told the toys what had happened, and everyone was very sad.

The next night the goblins visited the playroom bold as ever – and do you know, although the toys kept a close watch on them to make sure they did not take anything, those clever goblins managed to steal quite a lot of things.

"Look!" cried the walking duck, peeping into Mummy's work-basket, which she had left in the corner on the floor. "Mummy's little scissors are gone – the ones she cuts buttonholes with!"

"And all her needles!" cried the rabbit, seeing the needle-case quite empty.

"And her nice steel thimble," cried the clockwork mouse. "Oh, whatever will she say?"

"It is time *we* did some magic!" said the rabbit suddenly. "I believe I know how to get back the stolen things. Yes, I believe I do!"

He ran to the toy cupboard and pulled out a big magnet that the children sometimes played with. He and the toys slipped out of the window and ran to the oak tree. They banged on the door, and when the goblins opened it the toys crowded inside.

"Goblins," said the rabbit sternly, "we

have come to get back the things you stole tonight! We have some wonderful magic, much stronger than any *you* know! Watch!"

The rabbit took the big magnet, which he had been holding behind him, and showed it to the goblins. They laughed scornfully.

"That will not find you anything!" they said.

The rabbit held out the magnet, and then a very queer thing happened! The stolen pair of scissors, which had been hidden under the carpet, suddenly flew up to the magnet and hung themselves on the end of it! Then dozens of needles appeared and flew to the magnet, too! They hung there tightly. And then from a goblin's pocket the thimble flew out and rushed to the magnet as well.

"Aha!" said the rabbit, pleased. "You see what powerful magic we keep in the playroom, Goblins!"

The goblins turned pale, as they

stared in surprise. They had never seen a magnet before, and they were full of fear. They rushed to the door, crowded out, and disappeared into the night.

"We shan't see *them* again," said the rabbit pleased. "Let's just look round and see if we can find anything else they stole."

They hunted around and found all the things they had missed, and a few more, too! The walking duck took her key from the front door of the oak tree and tied it on to a new ribbon round her neck. She was very pleased to have it back again.

Then back they all went to the playroom and put the needles, thimble, and scissors into the work-basket. They laughed whenever they thought of the goblins' astonishment.

"That magnet was a fine idea," said the pink rabbit, putting it away in the cupboard. "I don't think the goblins will rob toys again. They will be too much afraid of magic in the playroom."

The riddling wizard

The riddling wizard wandered through the countryside, asking his odd riddles. If anyone could not answer, he made them pay him a golden piece.

So the country people were frightened when he came along, with his high pointed hat and his flowing cloak embroidered with shining suns, moons and stars.

He would stop on a village green, his big black cat beside him, and ring a loud bell. Everyone hurried to see what was the matter – and then the riddling wizard would get hold of someone and fire off his riddles.

They were always the same riddles, but no one could ever answer them.

In fact, no one believed they could be answered.

The first was this: "Pick up a stone from the ground. What tree will it grow into?"

The second was: "What creature has no wings and yet will fly through the air?"

The third was: "Bring me an apple that does not grow on an apple tree!"

As Jinky said, no one could answer riddles like that. "You can pick up as many stones as you like, but not one will ever grow into a tree! And how can anything fly if it has no wings? And who ever heard of an apple that did not grow on an apple tree?"

"It's an easy way for the riddling wizard to get money," grumbled Binny, the pixie. "He just asks his silly riddles and then fines us a gold piece!"

But after a while the riddling wizard got something more than a gold piece, as he wandered about. He made into servants all those who could not answer his riddles, and soon he had a train of miserable people following him, the black cat at the head.

Then the people of the countryside began to get really alarmed. They held a meeting. What were they to do about the riddling wizard?

"He's so powerful," said Kirry. "If we defy him, he will use his strong magic and turn us into hens that peck round his heels, or into snowflakes that melt in the sun, or mice for his black cat to hunt."

"What would happen if anyone answered his riddles?" asked Jiminy, a small goblin with a merry face.

"The person who can answer his riddles has the right also to ask the wizard three riddles," said Kirry. "He has said that if he cannot answer them, he will give his magic wand to his questioner. But that will never happen, because no one can answer his riddles, and certainly no one could ever ask him riddles he couldn't answer. He is very wise and very clever."

"Well, if he comes here *I* will try to answer his riddles, and ask him some of my own," said Jiminy boldly. The others stared at him.

"You are foolish," said Jinky. "You will have to pay him a gold piece – and you know you have only one, Jiminy – and you will have to follow him as his servant for the rest of your life!"

"All the same, I will try to answer his riddles!" said Jiminy. "So when he comes, let me know."

In two weeks' time there came word that the riddling wizard was coming to Jiminy's village. The people there were alarmed and excited. Jiminy was the only calm one.

"Don't be afraid," he said. "I will be the one to face him, so if anyone has to pay him and follow him it will be I, Jiminy, and not any of you!"

The riddling wizard came. He stood on the village green, with his large black cat blinking her green eyes beside him. Behind him was his miserable train of servants, who were kept close to him by magic and could never run away.

The people came out of their houses. Jiminy was the first. It was he who faced the riddling wizard, and looked boldly at him. The wizard looked at Jiminy, and felt that it would be good to take money from this bold goblin and force him to wander behind him for miles.

"So you want to answer my riddles?" he said in his deep soft voice to Jiminy. "Then riddle me this! Pick up a stone from the ground. What tree will it grow into?"

Everyone watched Jiminy breathlessly. The goblin looked down on the ground, and then suddenly picked up something there. It was a cherry stone, dropped by someone who had sat on the green that morning, eating cherries!

"Here is a stone from the ground," said

Jiminy. "It will grow into a cherry tree!"

The wizard frowned. That was smart of Jiminy. Yes – it was a cherry stone – so certainly it could grow into a cherry tree, if it was planted. The wizard asked his next riddle.

"What creature has no wings and yet will fly through the air?"

Jiminy looked into a nearby bush, where he knew many caterpillars lived. He picked a caterpillar from the leaf it was eating and showed it to the wizard.

"Here is a creature that has no wings, and yet will fly – for it will change into a butterfly and wing its way through the air!"

Everyone clapped and cheered. How clever Jiminy was!

The wizard was not pleased, but he knew the answer was good. He asked the third riddle.

"Bring me an apple that does not grow on an apple tree!"

Jiminy crossed to an oak tree whose shady branches spread over the green.

He pulled a hard brown thing from a twig. It was an oak apple!

"Here is an apple that does not grow on an apple tree!" he cried, and threw the oak apple at the wizard in triumph. "Now I will riddle *you* three riddles! First, show me what goes as fast as the wind and yet makes no sound!"

"Easy!" cried the wizard, and before the astonished eyes of everyone he changed himself into a floating cloud, blown by the wind!

"Good!" cried Jiminy. "Now show me something so small I may hold it in my hand, and which yet contains something far bigger than I am!"

"Easy!" cried the wizard, and changed himself into an acorn which jumped into Jiminy's hand. Then, in a trice the wizard was himself again, and the acorn had vanished. "Was I not so small I was in your hand – and yet does not an acorn contain an oak tree?"

"Good," said Jiminy. "Now for my third riddle. Show me something that is often whipped hard and yet does no wrong!"

"Easy!" said the wizard, and changed himself into a pool of rich cream. Everyone stared and laughed. Yes, cream could be whipped, and yet did no wrong! Alas, the wizard had answered all the goblin's riddles.

Jiminy had guessed that the wizard would turn himself into a pool of cream. Quick as lightning the goblin called out to the wizard's big black cat. "Puss! There's your dinner!"

The black cat stared at the cream in surprise. She ran to it eagerly, and began to lap it up. A voice came from it.

"Stop! Stop! Let me change myself back to my own shape."

The cat took no notice. She lapped up all the cream, and then sat down and began to wash herself. Everyone stood silent for a moment. The wizard did not come back. He was gone. He had been licked up. Oh, clever Jiminy!

Everyone patted him and praised him, and the wizard's captives cheered and pranced about, for now they were free. Oh, clever Jiminy!

"You can have the wizard's wand!" they cried, and picked it up. "Then, if he manages to come back, he will be in your power."

The wizard never did come back, which was a good thing. The black cat settled down happily with Jiminy. Jiminy still has the wand, but he uses it for good magic and not for bad. He was clever, wasn't he? Could *you* have answered the wizard's riddles, do you think?

The enchanted gloves

Ho-Ho and Higgledy were two little brownies who lived in Sunflower Cottage on the edge of Honey Common. One was a painter and the other was a carpenter. Ho-Ho could paint a wall or a door in double-quick time, and Higgledy could make anything you pleased, from a giant's table to a canary's bath.

One day they had a message from Long-Beard the Chancellor of Fairyland. He lived in a palace nearby, and the two brownies often saw him out in his golden carriage.

Ho-Ho opened the letter, and read it out loud to Higgledy. This is what it said:

"The Chancellor would be glad if Ho-

Ho and Higgledy would call at his palace tomorrow morning to do some work."

"Ha!" said Higgledy, pleased. "That's fine! We shall get well paid for that! And it will be lovely to say that we work for the Chancellor. All our friends will know then that we are good workmen."

The next morning the brownies went to the palace. Long-Beard the Chancellor saw them, and told them that he wanted his dining room painted yellow and a new bookshelf made for his study.

"Very good, sir," said Ho-Ho and Higgledy. "We will start straight away."

They began their work, whistling merrily. Cinders, the Chancellor's black cat, and Snowie, his white dog, came to watch them. They sat solemnly there watching everything the brownies did.

"Do go away," said Ho-Ho at last. "You make us feel quite uncomfortable, staring all day like that."

"We like to watch you," said Cinders. "What a lovely colour that yellow is, Ho-Ho."

"I wish my tail was that colour," said Snowie the dog. "I hate being all white, and I think Snowie is such a silly name."

"Well, it's just as bad being all black," said Cinders. "It's very dull. Now if I were striped yellow I should feel grand."

"Will you have any paint left over when you have finished your job, Ho-Ho?" asked the dog.

"I might," said Ho-Ho. "But if you think I'm going to waste it on you, you're very much mistaken."

"Yes, but the Chancellor would be so pleased," said Cinders. "I'm sure he's tired of seeing us all one colour. He might pay you double for being so kind."

"I don't know about that," said Higgledy. "I've heard the Chancellor isn't very generous."

"Snowie! Cinders! Come and have your dinners!" called a voice. The two animals ran off and Ho-Ho and Higgledy went on with their work.

The next day and the next, Snowie and Cinders came and watched the two brownies. On the third day, when Ho-Ho had finished painting the walls a beautiful bright yellow and Higgledy had made a very nice bookcase, the two animals went over to the paint jar. They looked into it and then spoke to Ho-Ho.

"Ho-Ho, *do* let us have the little bit of paint that's left," begged Cinders. "We would be glad of it and we are sure the Chancellor would be pleased. Couldn't you just paint us yellow with your big brush? Do! Do!"

"Please!" said Snowie, wagging his tail hard. "How would you like to be dressed in nothing but white all your life long?"

"I shouldn't like it at all," said Ho-Ho. "But I don't know whether I dare do what you want."

The animals begged so hard that at last Ho-Ho and Higgledy gave in. Higgledy painted Snowie's long tail a most beautiful yellow, and gave him yellow ears too, and Ho-Ho painted long yellow stripes all down Cinders' black body.

They did look funny. Ho-Ho and Higgledy began to laugh when they saw how strange the two animals looked. But Cinders and Snowie were pleased. They ran out of the room and down the passage, and just round the corner they met the Chancellor.

He stared in astonishment and horror at his cat and dog. Whatever could have happened to them? Was this really Snowie, with yellow ears and tail?

What a horrible-looking animal! And could this really be his beautiful black cat, Cinders, with long yellow stripes all down his body?

"My eyes must be going wrong!" groaned the Chancellor. "Where are my glasses?"

He put them on and looked at the animals again – but they were still the same. What a terrible thing!

"Who has done this dreadful deed?" roared the Chancellor, suddenly feeling very angry. "Ho-Ho and Higgledy, is it you?"

He strode into the dining room and found the two brownies there, looking rather scared.

"How dare you paint my cat and dog!" shouted Long-Beard. "Get out of my palace at once!"

"But please, sir, Snowie and Cinders begged and begged us to," said Ho-Ho, trembling. "We didn't want to do it, but they said you would be pleased."

"I don't believe you!" said the

Chancellor, angrily. "You did it for a horrid joke. Go away at once and never come back!"

"We've finished our work," said Ho-Ho, "so we will go if you will kindly pay us, sir."

"Pay you!" cried the Chancellor. "Not a penny piece! Not a penny piece! Ho there, servants! Come and throw these wicked brownies out."

Two servants at once ran up, caught hold of the brownies, and threw them down the front steps of he palace. Ho-Ho and Higgledy picked themselves up and ran off in fright, leaving behind all their tools and brushes.

They didn't stop running till they came to Sunflower Cottage. Then they sat down in their little chairs and wept bitterly.

"Nasty, horrid old Chancellor!" said Ho-Ho. "We did our work. Why couldn't he have paid us? He just wanted to save the money, the mean old thing!"

"We'll pay him back somehow!" said

Higgledy, drying his eyes. "We'll go to Thumbs, the glove-maker. He's very clever, and perhaps he will think of some way to punish the mean Chancellor."

So next day they went to visit their friend, Thumbs. He made gloves – red ones, white ones, brown ones, blue ones, little and big, thin and thick. He was very clever indeed.

"Welcome!" he said, when he saw his two friends. He put down his work and set out three cups and three plates. "We will have some biscuits and cocoa. You look sad. Tell me your trouble."

So over their steaming cups of cocoa, Ho-Ho and Higgledy told Thumbs all about the mean Chancellor, and how he had thrown them out of the palace without paying them a penny just because they had been kind enough to do what Snowie and Cinders had begged them to do.

"We mean to punish the Chancellor, but we can't think how," said Higgledy.

"You are clever, Thumbs. Can you help us?"

Thumbs put his finger on his nose and rubbed it, thinking hard. Then he began to smile.

"I've got an idea!" he said. "It's old Long-Beard's birthday next week. I'll make him a pair of gloves and you can send them to him without saying where they come from. Inside the gloves I'll put a naughty spell. This spell will act as soon as he puts the gloves on."

"What will it do?" asked Ho-Ho in excitement.

"Why, it will make him pinch, punch and pull anybody who happens to be with him at the time!" said Thumbs. "Both his hands will act so strangely he won't know what is happening! They will pull people's noses, box their ears, tickle their ribs and pinch them! Goodness, how funny it would be to watch!"

Ho-Ho, Higgledy and Thumbs began to laugh till the tears ran down their noses and dropped into their cocoa. Oh, what a joke it would be!

All that week Thumbs worked at the gloves. They were beautiful, deep red with little yellow buttons and edged with white fur.

When the right day came Ho-Ho and Higgledy posted the parcel to Long-Beard. They decided to take a walk near the palace on the afternoon of the Chancellor's birthday, to see if they could hear what had happened.

Long-Beard had scores of parcels on his birthday. He opened them one after another, and most of them he didn't like a bit, for he was a mean old man. But when he came to the gloves — oh, my! What a fine surprise! What magnificent gloves! How warm! Who could have sent them? There was no card in the parcel and Long-Beard puzzled his head to think who could have given him such a nice present.

"It must be the King himself!" he thought at last. "He thinks a lot of me, and I expect he has sent me these gloves to show me how much he likes me. Well, I must wear them this afternoon, that's certain, for the King is calling for me in his carriage, and he will like to see his present on my hands."

So that afternoon, when the King's carriage rolled up at exactly three o'clock, the Chancellor stood ready. He carried his new gloves in his hand, intending to put them on as soon as he was in the carriage, so that the King would see them and perhaps say that he had sent them.

The King leaned out to greet his Chancellor.

"Come into the carriage, Long-Beard," he said. "It is a beautiful afternoon for a drive and we have a good deal of business to arrange."

Long-Beard stepped in and the door was closed. Just then up came Ho-Ho, Higgledy and Thumbs, out for a walk near the palace. Seeing the Chancellor getting into the King's carriage with the enchanted gloves in his hand they stood still in fright. Whatever would happen to the King when Long-Beard put on his gloves?

"Come on, we must go with the carriage!" cried Ho-Ho, and he ran after it. All three brownies swung themselves up on the ledge behind the carriage and sat there, unseen by anyone.

The Chancellor put on his gloves and the King looked at them.

"What beautiful gloves," he said – and then he gave a shout of surprise!

For Long-Beard's hands suddenly flew to the King's nose and pulled it hard! Then they went to the King's ribs and began to tickle him!

"Ooh!" cried the King. "Ooh! Stop it! Whatever is the matter with you, Long-Beard? Have you gone mad?"

The Chancellor was filled with horror. What was he doing? Why did his hands do such dreadful things? Why, they were boxing the King's ears now! He

tried to put them into his pockets, but he couldn't. They flew to the King's head, knocked his crown off and pulled his hair! Then they pinched his cheeks!

The King grew angry, and pinched the Chancellor back. Then he gave him a push that made the Chancellor gasp. The three brownies saw all that happened, for they were peeping in at the windows and they were horrified.

"Gloves, come to me!" cried Thumbs, suddenly.

At once the red gloves flew off Long-Beard's hands and went to Thumbs. The Chancellor's hands stopped behaving so strangely, and he stared at the King in shame.

The King stopped the carriage and got out.

"I must get to the bottom of this," he said. "What explanation have you, Long-Beard?"

"None, Your Majesty," said Long-Beard, trembling. "I don't know how it happened at all."

"Well, perhaps *you* can tell me the meaning of this!" said the King, turning suddenly to the three brownies, who stood nearby, red-faced and ashamed.

"Please, Your Majesty, I will confess everything," said Ho-Ho, and he told the King all that had happened – about the work done at Long-Beard's palace, the cat and the dog painted yellow, and the Chancellor's anger and meanness. Then he told how Thumbs had made the gloves to punish Long-Beard. The King looked stern.

"You had no right to think you could punish the Chancellor yourselves," he said. "You should have come to me and made your complaint. You have done wrong, and you must be punished. As for the Chancellor, he did wrong too, but he has been punished enough. He must certainly pay you what he owes you, but you must give half of it to the brownies' hospital. And you must polish my carriage until it sparkles."

So the three brownies had to spend all

day polishing the King's carriage. Then the King forgave them. The Chancellor opened his purse and with very bad grace gave Ho-Ho and Higgledy what he owed them.

"You might give me ten pounds to put in the hospital box too," said the King to the angry Chancellor. "I'm sure it wouldn't hurt you."

The three brownies walked home, not knowing whether to be glad or sorry.

"We'd better not be naughty any more," said Ho-Ho at last, "or listen to any more cats and dogs. What do you think, Higgledy and Thumbs?"

"We agree," said his friends. So for quite half a year they were as good as gold. And after that – ah, but that's another story!

The magic bubble pipes

Merry and Bright were hard at work making their famous bubble pipes. They were pretty little pipes, carved neatly round the bowl, and the brownies sold them for a penny each. Merry and Bright sold hundreds of them, for the fairies loved to blow bubbles. Sometimes the little people sailed off on a big one, and sometimes they took their little scissors and snipped pieces off the brightest coloured bubbles to make into dresses and coats.

Now one day Dame Tiptap came along and looked at the little pipes. She didn't want to buy one, but she liked to stand and watch the two little

brownies making them.

Merry and Bright thought she was a funny old dame.

"Do you want a pipe to smoke, Dame Tiptap?" asked Merry.

"Of course not," said the old lady angrily. "You know I would never dream of smoking a pipe. Don't be rude!"

"Have a look at this one, Dame Tiptap," said Bright, and he held up a long-stemmed pipe to the old lady. It was filled with soapy water, but Dame Tiptap didn't know that. She put on her glasses to have a look, for she thought the pipe must be a special one.

"Smell it," said Bright, with a giggle. Dame Tiptap bent closer and smelled it, and at that very moment Bright blew hard down the stem of the pipe, and some soapy bubbles rose out of the bowl and burst in the old lady's face. What a fright she got! She nearly fell over, and how those two rascally brownies roared to see her face covered all over with bubbles.

"That is very rude and unkind of you," said Dame Tiptap angrily. "You deserve to be punished for that." She took out a yellow box, and from it scattered a misty powder over the brownies' hands.

"There's a spell in that," she said, "and it's gone into your fingers now. Whatever you make will get a bit of the spell too, when the powder works. Ha, ha, Merry and Bright, you'll soon wish you hadn't played a trick on old Tiptap!"

Off she went, wiping her soapy face. The brownies looked at one another in dismay, and then looked at their hands. They seemed all right. Whatever could the spell be?

"Oh, it's just nothing," said Merry at last. "She was trying to frighten us, that's all."

They went on with their work and made dozens of bubble pipes that day, but the spell went into many of the pipes as they worked, and lay there until the right time came.

Twelve of the pipes had the spell. The rest were all right. The little people came to buy the pipes and took them home. They made soapy water and put the pipes to their mouths, and blew bubbles.

And then those pipes that had the spell in them began to act very strangely indeed! Even when the fairy stopped blowing, the soapy bubbles went on coming out of the pipe! Soon the room was full of bubbles, but still the pipe went on blowing them out. They floated out of the window. They floated through the wood, and then, one by one, they burst.

And, dear me, each bubble burst with a bang as loud as a gun going off. It made everyone jump nearly out of their skins, and the King cried, "Guns! Is that an enemy coming?"

Bang! Bang! Bang! The bubbles went

on bursting as they flew out of the pipes. The King and his courtiers sent orders to the army to turn out. It must be an enemy coming! Bang! BANG!

The army turned out, and aeroplanes buzzed overhead to see if they could find the enemy with so many guns. But not a sign of anyone could they see. Just then some of the bubbles, which had floated high in the air, burst near the aeroplanes. Bang! Bang! Pop! Bang!

"We are being shot at!" cried the pilots, and they raced downwards to tell the King. What a to-do there was! All that day, as the bubbles popped and banged, messengers rushed here and there trying to find out what was the matter, and the army marched north, south, east and west to stop the enemy that nobody could see.

And then, at last, bubbles floated into the palace garden, and the King saw that what he had thought was the banging of guns was really the popping of magic bubbles. How annoyed he was.

To think he had called out his army and his air force to fight a lot of bubbles!

It wasn't long before he had Merry and Bright before him and was asking them the meaning of such a thing. They were trembling, because they had not known that the spell would cause the pipes to go on pouring out bubbles, bubbles that banged like guns when they burst.

They told the King everything, and he sent for Dame Tiptap too. Merry and Bright felt ashamed of themselves when the old lady told of the trick they had played on her.

"You should not have blown such a powerful spell over their hands," said the King. "It has caused a great deal of trouble. Take the spell off their hands, Dame Tiptap."

"I can't, Your Majesty," said the old lady. "It is there for good."

"Well, they will have to put up with it, then," said the King. "But I doubt if anyone will buy their pipes now that they know what dreadful bubbles they blow. Take the magic pipes, Dame Tiptap, and destroy them. We cannot have them pouring out bubbles like this."

So the pipes were burnt, and the bang-bang-bang of bursting bubbles stopped. There was peace once more.

But Merry and Bright found that the King was right when he said that no one would want to buy their pipes any more. Everyone was too much afraid of getting an enchanted pipe. They didn't want that! So they went to the yellow goblin, who also sold pipes, and bought them from him, and Merry and Bright found that they were getting very poor indeed.

"What shall we do?" said Merry. But Bright didn't know. The two brownies could not do anything else but make pipes. They sat and looked as miserable as could be.

And then an old oak tree near by spoke to them.

"I will buy your pipes to put my acorns in," said the tree. "But as I have about a thousand acorns this year, I cannot pay you a penny for each of your pipes. I shall give you one penny for a hundred pipes. That's all."

"But we should have to work dreadfully, dreadfully hard then!" cried Merry.

"Hard work never hurt anyone," said the oak tree. "Well, take it or leave it. You'll find no one else buys your pipes now, and it surely is better to sell them at a penny a hundred than to have them falling to bits in your cupboard!"

Well, there was some sense in what the tree said, and the two brownies had to agree. But how hard they had to work now – and for such a little money too! They made the little pipes all day long, and at night they set the acorns neatly into them, so that each acorn had a little resting-place and did not easily fall off the tree when the wind blew. The oak tree made them carve the pipes neatly, just as before.

Merry and Bright are not quite so merry and bright now! But still, as the oak tree said, hard work never hurt anyone; and although the two brownies haven't nearly so much money as they used to have, they still have time to play now and again. You will usually see them in an oak wood, hard at work on their tiny pipes; and it is said that some of the pipes have that magic spell in them still, so if you want a bit of excitement, try blowing bubbles through a few of the acorn pipes and see if anything happens. You never know!

And don't forget to see how neatly Merry and Bright carve the bowls of their pipes, and how beautifully they make them to fit each acorn.

The Christmas pudding
wish

"Children! I'm making your Christmas pudding!" called Mummy. "It's all mixed. Do you want to come and stir it round, and wish your Christmas wish?"

"Oh *yes!*" shouted the three children and they came rushing into the kitchen. Mummy had a big bowl and in it was a glorious mixture. Big Peter took the spoon first and stirred hard. He wished hard too.

Then Alice stirred and wished. "And now it's your turn, Little Ben," said Mummy. Ben really was very small indeed. He had been ill a great many times and he just hadn't grown.

"Will my wish really come true?" he said.

"You never know!" said his mother. "Wish your very hardest!"

So Ben stirred the stiff mixture and he wished a wish to himself. "I wish I could see Father Christmas and help him!" He wished it three times for luck.

Now, on Christmas Eve the three children hung up their stockings, of course. Ben's was smaller than anyone's because his feet were tiny. He didn't think Father Christmas would be able to put much into it!

He went to bed – but he kept thinking of his Christmas pudding wish. *Would* it come true? Did pudding wishes ever come true?

"I must keep awake," thought Ben. "I can't expect my wish to come true if I'm asleep when Father Christmas comes!"

About twelve o'clock, when the house was dark and still, Ben went to the window. He thought he had heard a faraway jingling of bells. Yes – he had. And will you believe it, four reindeer came galloping through the sky, their bells jingling merrily. Ben watched in excitement.

And then, just as the sleigh was over Ben's garden, something fell out – something small that went tumbling down into the thick snow just outside Ben's window! Whatever could it be?

Then the reindeer stopped with a jerk, and to Ben's enormous delight the sleigh came down to earth in his garden – and in the moonlight he saw the big, burly figure of Father Christmas!

Father Christmas got out and went over to the little thing in the snow. "Are you hurt?" Ben heard him say. "Dear, dear – how silly of you to fall out like that!"

Ben was so excited that he began to shake. He must go and speak to Father Christmas, he must, he must! He pulled on his dressing-gown, tied a scarf round

his neck, and slipped down the stairs and out of the garden door. Soon he stood beside Father Christmas.

"Hallo there!" said Father Christmas, surprised. "What a tiny thing you are! Are you a pixie or something?"

"No. I'm a boy," said Ben. "What's happened?"

"A most annoying thing," said Father Christmas. "I brought this little imp with me to go down the chimneys instead of me this year. Somehow or other I've got a bit plump, and I'm afraid of getting stuck. And now the silly little creature has fallen out and hurt himself – he says he can't go climbing up and down chimneys tonight. And I'd like to know where I can get anyone small enough at a moment's notice!"

Well! *Ben* knew where he could get someone! He pulled at Father Christmas's sleeve. "Won't *I* do?" he said anxiously. "See how small I am! I could go down chimneys easily. Let me help you, do, do let me help you!"

"Right," said Father Christmas. "It's very good of you. Change clothes with the imp. He's got a black suit on, so that the soot won't show."

In two minutes Ben had the black suit on, and was sitting beside Father Christmas in the sleigh. What a treat! What a surprise! His Christmas pudding wish had come true!

Well, Ben found it easy to slip down chimneys and climb up again. He was very good and quick at stuffing stockings full of toys. He chuckled when he saw the sleeping children. What would they say if they woke up and saw who was filling their stockings *that* night?

He even filled Big Peter's stocking, and Alice's. But he didn't fill his own. He didn't quite like to do that. Anyway, what did it matter if his was empty in the morning? He would have had the most wonderful treat in the world!

Ben was very busy that night. The roofs they landed on! The chimneys he went down! The big and little stockings he filled! Father Christmas was delighted with him.

"Don't grow too big next year," he said. "I might want you again! Now – we've finished. Here we are back in your garden again. Change clothes with the imp."

They changed clothes. Ben rubbed the soft nose of each reindeer, gave Father Christmas a sudden hug and ran in through the garden door and up the stairs. He was very tired.

"I'm happy, I'm happy!" he said to himself as he got into bed. "Nobody will believe me tomorrow – but it's quite, quite true!"

In the morning what a surprise! Ben sat up in bed and the first thing he saw was his stocking full with toys from top to toe. They overflowed on to the bed and even on to the floor! He sat and stared at them.

Had he dreamt it all then? His stocking had been empty when he climbed into bed. Surely the imp hadn't been able to get down the chimney after all?

"I don't believe my wish *did* come true," thought Ben, sadly. "I've just had a lovely dream. Oh, I *do* feel so disappointed!"

But wait – what was this? Ben, Ben, look at your hands! Black with soot! Where did *that* come from? Ben gave a squeal of joy.

"It *was* true! I've helped Father Christmas – and somehow my stocking has been filled too! It's ALL true!"

Wasn't it strange the way his Christmas pudding wish came true? Do you ever wish when you stir the Christmas pudding? You do? Well, let me know if your wish comes true, like Ben's, won't you?

I do hope it does.

Go and dig potatoes!

O nce, when little Dame Hurry was
walking over the common with her
shopping in a basket, she heard a lark
singing. It was singing so beautifully
that she looked up to see where it was.

"Your music pours down like rain!"
she called to the lark. She hurried
on her way, still looking up at the
singing lark, high in the blue sky.
She didn't see a rabbit-hole. She put
her little foot right into it and fell
over.

She gave a scream. "Oh, my ankle,
my ankle! I've sprained it. Oh, the pain!
Help, help!"

Poor little Dame Hurry sat on the
grass and nursed her foot. She couldn't

stand on it because it hurt her so. All her shopping was spilt from her basket. Dear, dear, and her Aunt Lollipop was coming to dinner.

"Help!" called Dame Hurry, hoping that someone would hear her. "Help!"

Somebody did hear her. It was Grabbit the Goblin. He came over to Dame Hurry, and she told him what she had done. "Could you help me home, please?" she asked. "And pick up my shopping for me?"

"I shall want something in return for my trouble," said Grabbit, who was mean and unkind.

"Oh, can't you help me just out of kindness?" said Dame Hurry. "It's so much nicer to do things for that reason, if you can."

"Pooh! Kindness! Not me," said Grabbit rudely. "Well, if you can't give me a reward for helping you, I'm off. No one else is likely to come by today, so you'll be here all day – and all night, too, I shouldn't wonder!"

"How mean you are," said Dame Hurry. "But don't go, please don't go. I really must get home before my Aunt Lollipop comes. I'll give you ten pence for your trouble."

"No, I don't want that," said Grabbit, looking suddenly very sly. "I want something else. Lend me your magic spade for a week."

"Certainly not!" said Dame Hurry. "What, lend my precious magic to *you*? I wouldn't dream of it."

"Right, then! I'm going," said Grabbit, and took a step away. Dame Hurry began to cry. "All right, all right, you mean creature. I'll lend you my spade for a week, and much good may it do you!"

"It will!" said Grabbit. "It can dig up all my potatoes for me! Ho, ho! It will save me a lot of work, I can tell you."

He helped Dame Hurry to her feet, after he had picked up her shopping. Then he helped her home. Her Aunt Lollipop had already arrived, and ran to bathe Dame Hurry's poor swollen foot.

"What about that spade?" said Grabbit. "I want it now."

"Oh dear, oh dear, can't you even wait till my foot is bathed?" said Dame Hurry. "Well, you will find it in the garden shed. But, listen, Grabbit, you will have to speak to the spade politely and kindly, and you must always clean it when it has been working for you."

"Pooh!" said Grabbit, rudely, and went off to get the spade. It was rather a peculiar one, for it had no proper handle, but a very big steel piece for digging. Grabbit picked it up, put it over his shoulder, and went home.

He stuck the spade into the ground. "Go and dig potatoes," he commanded. The spade hopped over to a potato patch and set to work. It was marvellous to see it digging away by itself.

"Hey! Sort the potatoes out nicely," said Grabbit to the spade. "Don't fling them here, there and everywhere. Big ones together, and middle-sized ones, and small ones, do you hear?"

The spade dug so violently that one of the potatoes shot up in the air and hit Grabbit on the head. He growled and went indoors.

The spade finished digging up that patch of potatoes. It hopped into the kitchen to be cleaned. But Grabbit wasn't going to bother to do that!

"Go and stand in the shed," he ordered the spade. "*I'm* not going to bother to clean you."

The spade hopped out, making a tremendous noise as if it was cross. Grabbit went to sleep.

Next day he ordered the spade to dig up a weedy patch of garden for him. "And do it properly!" he said. "Get the weeds up by the roots. Go on, dig!"

The spade dug. It flung up the weeds so high that bits of earth flew all over Grabbit. He went indoors, frowning. As soon as he had gone into the house the spade went over to the fence and leaned itself there. It didn't do any more digging at all.

When Grabbit came out and found that the spade had done hardly any digging, he lost his temper. "I'll put you on the rubbish heap! You'll do what I say or you'll be sorry!"

He didn't clean the spade that day, either. It went to its place in the shed so dirty that there wasn't one single shiny bit to be seen. It scraped itself angrily along the floor.

The next day, Grabbit wanted to go and do some shopping. He called to the spade first. "Go and dig potatoes! Dig and dig and dig! Don't you dare to stop digging once you begin. Go and dig potatoes!"

The spade hopped out to a very big potato patch and began to dig. It was afraid of Grabbit. Suppose he really did put it on the rubbish heap?

Grabbit went out shopping. He met some friends and was a very long time gone. The spade dug up all the potatoes and sorted them out carefully.

Then it wondered where Grabbit was and went to look for him in the kitchen. No Grabbit. Well, well, Grabbit had told the spade to dig and dig and dig, and not stop, so the spade thought it had better obey.

It went out into the garden and dug up all the rose-trees. Then it dug up the onions. Then it went to the lawn and dug up all the grass.

Well, there was no garden to dig after that. What could the spade do next? It had to dig and dig and dig!

It dug up the fence. That was a hard job, and the spade enjoyed it. Then it dug up the garden shed. My, that was a fine job for a magic spade! It dug so hard that it almost panted.

Still Grabbit wasn't back. So the spade began to dig up Grabbit's cottage. It dug and it dug, heaving itself

underneath it, and soon the cottage began to topple over on one side. The spade was pleased.

Then Grabbit came back. He was shocked to see his cottage toppling over. He was horrified to see his garden shed lying on its side. He couldn't believe his eyes when he saw his fence dug up – and his lawn – and his roses. He must be in a dream!

But he wasn't. It was quite, quite true. He rushed at the hard-working spade with a shout – but it hopped away at once, and went back to Dame Hurry.

Grabbit went crying round to Dame Hurry, too. "Come and see the damage your horrid magic spade has done. It has dug up my fence and shed and my house, too! You'll have to pay me for all that!"

"Indeed I shan't," said Dame Hurry. "You can put everything right yourself. It's all your own fault. And if you say another word, I'll *give* you the spade, Grabbit – and maybe it will start digging you up, too!"

"I wish I'd helped you out of kindness now," wept Grabbit. "I wish I had. I wouldn't have brought all this trouble on myself then."

"Ah, no luck comes to those who have to be paid for doing a bit of kindness," said Dame Hurry. "No luck at all. Just you remember that, Grabbit."

The Ho-Ho goblins

O nce upon a time the Ho-Ho goblins laid a plan. They wanted to catch the Skippetty pixies, but for a long time they hadn't been able even to get near them. Now they had thought of a marvellous idea!

"Listen!" said Snicky, the head goblin. "You know when the pixies sit down to feast, in the middle of their dancing, don't you? Well, they sit on toadstools! And if *we* grow those toadstools we can put a spell in them so that as soon as the pixies sit down on them, they shoot through the earth into our caves below – and we shall have captured them."

"A splendid idea!" said the other

goblins in delight. "We'll do it!"

"Leave it all to me," said Snicky. "I will go to them and offer to grow them toadstools for their dance much more cheaply than anyone else."

He went knocking at the door of Pinky, one of the chief pixies.

"Dear Madam Pinky," said Snicky, bowing low, "I come to ask you if you will kindly allow me to grow the toadstools for you for your dance."

"How much do you charge?" asked Pinky.

"One gold piece for one hundred toadstools," said Snicky.

"That is very cheap," said Pinky. "Very well. You shall make them."

Snicky ran off full of glee. He had got what he wanted! He called a meeting of the others, and told them.

"Now," he said, "not one of you must tell a word of this to anyone, for we must keep it a secret. We must get a runaway spell from Witch Grumple, and each toadstool must be rubbed with the spell. Then, at a magic word, all the toadstools, with the pixies on them, will rush away through the ground straight to our caves below."

"Hurrah!" cried the Ho-Ho goblins. "They will be our servants at last."

Snicky went to ask Witch Grumple for the spell.

"Good evening, Witch Grumple," said Snicky. "May I speak secretly with you for a moment?"

"Certainly," said the witch. She looked all around to see that no one was about. "Come into the corn," she said. "No one will hear us then. What is it you want?"

"I want a runaway spell," said Snicky.

"What will you give me for it?" asked the witch.

"I'll give you two Skippetty pixies for servants," said Snicky.

"Don't be silly," said Grumple. "You haven't any pixies to give away!"

"I soon shall have if you let me have the runaway spell," said Snicky.

"Tell me what you are going to do with it," said Grumple.

"No," said Snicky, "someone might hear me."

"There is no one to hear you," said Grumple. "Tell me, or I will not let you have the spell."

So Snicky told Grumple exactly what he was going to do to capture the pixies, and she shook with laughter.

"Splendid!" she said. "I shall be glad to see those stuck-up little pixies punished. Come back with me and I'll give you the spell."

Now all would have gone well with the Ho-Ho goblin's plan – if someone hadn't overheard the secret that Snicky told Grumple. Who heard it? You will never guess.

The corn heard it with their many, many ears! They listened to all that Snicky said, and, because they liked the Skippetty pixies, they wanted to warn them. So the next time the wind blew the corn, it whispered its secret to the breeze.

"Shish-a-shish-a-shish-a-shish!" went the corn as the wind blew over it. The wind understood its language and listened in astonishment to the tale the corn told of Snicky's plan. Off it went to the pixies at once.

When Pinky heard of Snicky's plan, she went pale with rage and fear. To think how that horrid, horrid goblin had nearly tricked her! Off she sped to the Fairy King and told him everything. He laughed and said, "Aha! Now we shall be able to play a nice little trick on Snicky himself!"

So, on the night of the dance, all the pixies laughed and talked as if they had no idea of the toadstool trick. The goblins crept around, watching and waiting for the moment when they could send the toadstools rushing down below to their caves.

Suddenly Pinky stopped the dance and said, "Let's play musical chairs for a change! Goblins, come and play with us!"

Pinky pointed to the toadstools that Snicky had grown for them.

"Those shall be the chairs," she said. "When the music stops, everyone must sit down if he can!"

The band began again. Pixies and goblins ran merrily round the toadstools – but every pixie had been warned not to sit down, but to let the goblins take the toadstools. So, when the music stopped, the goblins made a rush for the toadstools and sat down on them.

As soon as Pinky saw the goblins sitting on the toadstools, she called out a magic word at the top of her voice. Those toadstools sank down through the ground at top speed!

To the goblins' great fright, the toadstools rushed down to their cave – and there, calmly waiting for them, were the soldiers of the Fairy King. As the toadstools came to rest in the caves, each goblin was surrounded by three soldiers. They were prisoners!

"That was a fine trick you planned,

wasn't it?" grinned a soldier. "But not so fine when it's played on yourselves! Come along now, quick march!"

Off the goblins went — and for a whole year they had to work hard for the pixies, to punish them for trying to play such a horrid trick.

And to this day they don't know who gave their secret away — although people say that if you listen to the corn as it whispers in the wind, you can, if you have sharp ears, hear it telling the wind all about Witch Grumple and Snicky the goblin. I'd love to hear it, wouldn't you?